Letter to a Younger Son

Find a way or make one.
Seneca

By the same author

Novels

The Wheel
A Portion of the Wilderness
O Stranger the World
The Long Play
The Send Off
The Everything Man
The Pheasant Shoot

Short stories

Scars and Other Ceremonies

Letter
to a
Younger Son

Christopher Leach

J. M. Dent & Sons Ltd
London, Melbourne and Toronto

First published 1981
© Christopher Leach, 1981

Printed in Great Britain by
Biddles Ltd, Guildford for
J. M. Dent & Sons Ltd
Aldine House, 33 Welbeck Street, London

Set in 12 on 14 point Monophoto Times by
Northampton Phototypesetters Ltd

British Library Cataloguing in Publication Data

Leach, Christopher
    Letter to a younger son.
    1. Bereavement – Psychological aspects
    2. Father and child
    I. Title
    301.42′86   BF575.G7

    ISBN 0–460–04496–6

To
Martin

Part One

What is death?
I don't know.
But you are a Zen Master!
Yes, but I am not a dead Zen Master.

1

A year ago I stood in the curve of this window and looked out into the garden where you and Jonathan were playing. Working together, you and he had built an assault-course of planks and bricks on the lawn, and were hurtling your bikes through it at speeds that made me wince. I opened the window and told you to be careful. You both paused, nodded and waved – and went faster.

And, as I continued to watch you, the thought came out of nowhere: supposing I were to die on this instant, *now,* my hand slipping from the catch, the garden darkening – what would you know of the man who had called and warned; what would you know of his opinions, his beliefs; the past that had made him what he was: this man who had helped you into life – your father?

True, you had my books. But, being fiction, they showed only the themes that interested me, my preoccupations. What did you know of the inner man? Even less than myself. And, were I to die now, you would have few memories, growing fainter with time, and changing in the telling.

My own father had died when I was eleven: a grandfather you have never seen; an ancestor you will never know. What memories I have of him are mainly visual: a dark figure at the top of the stairs, calling; the scar on his right wrist, livid, burning, where shrapnel had entered and passed through in France in 1917; straw gleaming like splintered sunlight on his horse-smelling jacket; the figure that loomed out of the pub's warmth on winter afternoons, refusing to come home; and then coming home, that heavy hand on my shoulder, the studded boots sparking; the bowed man sitting on the edge of his bed, fighting a smoker's cough that rattled his body every morning, early.

I knew he loved watching football; that he liked his drink; that he was contemptuous of bad weather and illness, until they humbled him; that he laughed at the idea of death, until death claimed him in a public ward, and he wept over a rack of bones that was no longer his body. But of the essential man I know nothing. Even his features are a blur – the only photograph that of a thin youth posed stiffly between tall plants and against a romantic sepia landscape: an unlined, unformed face.

I did not want you and Jonathan to know so little about me. I wanted to tell you then, as I looked out of this window a year ago, who I was, before it was too late; and, in the process, discover more about myself, for myself. And so I decided to write a book for you both. I would call it *A LETTER TO MY SONS*. I was busy with other commissions, but I told myself I would write it soon – perhaps within the year. I savoured the prospect: seeing the finished book in my mind's eye, holding it in my hands: the binding, the new, tacky pages – for you, and for me. I tried out first sentences. I felt it grow. Soon I would begin. It glowed in the distance: a warm light, coming nearer. *Soon* – I told myself.

Until the night of the second of February, nineteen hundred and seventy-nine; and the chill morning of the third . . .

2

You said: 'Can we go in the bath together?'

I looked at you both, standing in front of the fire: you, at ten, tall, dark, long-boned like myself: a potential six-footer; Jonathan, almost twelve, fair, slighter, more nervously aware, always the leader in imaginary games, prone in recent years to asthma. I thought of the usual aftermath to that request: the laughter that would grow to shrieks; the bathroom awash; towels soaked; a slippery avalanche of naked bodies down the stairs.

'No,' I said.

'Oh come on, Dad,' you said. 'We won't make a mess.'

'That's what you always say.'

'Promise.'

'Okay,' I said. 'But if I . . .'

'Thanks, Dad!'

And you were out of your clothes, and racing upstairs.

Promises or no, the shrieks grew. I heard sounds like the fall of giant waves. I gave you another ten minutes; then went up. The usual soaking chaos. I sent you down.

You dried yourselves in front of the fire, and I was proud of your lean bodies. You got into your pyjamas. You sat with me, one on either side of the armchair, watching TV while your mother made a last drink.

'Bed,' I said, later.

'Let's stay up,' said Jonathan. 'It's Saturday tomorrow: no school.'

'Another quarter of an hour,' I said. 'No more.'

When it was time to go, you both kissed your mother,

and I took you up. I came out of your room, and went into Jonathan's.

'Have you got your inhalers?' I said.

He took them from under his pillow.

'Okay,' I said. 'Goodnight.'

'Is Bobby in?' he said, naming his favourite of our two cats.

'No,' I lied. I did not approve of animals sharing a bed.

'If he comes in, will you bring him up?'

'Yes,' I lied again.

'Thanks. Goodnight, Dad.'

I went downstairs. Half an hour later you and he were still talking, room to room. I went to the bottom of the stairs and shut you up.

'Goodnight, Dad!'

'See you in the morning,' I said.

Your mother went to bed around eleven. I stayed watching TV until past midnight. On the way to my own bedroom I looked in on you both. The light from the landing illuminating your sleeping faces; then darkness.

The end of another normal day: the Art Room; my quota of writing completed; meals made and served and eaten; laughter and TV.

Yet nothing would ever be the same . . .

3

He had called before in the middle of the night – a sudden attack, a nightmare, a need to be reassured – but never with such urgency. Always a light sleeper, I was awake in an instant, staring into the dark. I heard him running along the landing towards my room, and then the door crashed back, bringing light. He stood there, his mouth wide, his body taut, one hand grasping an inhaler.

'I can't . . . breathe!' he said.

He threw himself on the bed, and turned on his back, a strange, soft, and terrible crowing coming from his throat.

I was out of bed now, and so was your mother.

'I'll go and get one of his pills,' she said, and ran out of the room.

He came forward, convulsively, off the bed.

'Want . . .' he began, and moved out of my hands towards the door.

'What do you want?'

'I want . . .' he said, and gestured towards the bathroom.

I half-ran, half-carried him there. There was no sound from your room: you slept on. Inside the bathroom we were too late: his bowels loosed; and then he fell. Your mother returned with the pills, and put the bottle above the basin. We cleaned the mess from his legs, and I carried him into his bedroom. He was unconscious now, breathing shallowly.

'He can't take the pill,' I said. 'Get the suppositories.'

They were supposed to work faster than the pill; and when she returned one was pressed into his anus, and we turned him over. We had never known anything as severe as this. Still half-asleep, we looked down at him: our son, your brother. Silence, save for the soft shuttle of his breath.

She had picked up his inhaler.

'It's empty,' she said.

Had he woken from a nightmare, and there, in the dark, inhaled too much? Was that possible? What fear, what combination of circumstances had brought on so fierce an attack?

Still he did not stir.

'I'll phone for an ambulance,' she said, and, once again, ran downstairs. I heard her soft, swift words.

'They're on their way,' she called.

I pressed my head against his chest. His heart beat on.

How many minutes passed? No one can say. You still slept on. Your mother waited downstairs. It was a bitterly cold winter's night: ice was thick on the cobbles of the courtyard. I decided to take Jonathan downstairs, where the last embers of a fire warmed the living-room. I wrapped a blanket around him, and lifted. As I entered the living-room, the phone rang. It was the ambulance crew: they had lost their way – our house was always hard to find, not isolated, but hidden away among farm-land. She re-directed them, and put down the receiver.

'I think I'd better get the doctor, too,' she said.

I nodded, stepping back from the sofa.

Our own doctor was not on duty that night; but another said he would come as soon as possible.

She took her coat from the hook and wrapped a scarf around her head.

'I'll go out and meet the ambulance,' she said.

I nodded again, and went back into the living-room. I looked down at Jonathan, a loop of fair hair across his forehead. Someone would have to go with him in the ambulance. I raced upstairs, and hurriedly got dressed.

As I came downstairs, pulling my sweater into place, lights from the ambulance whitened the courtyard, and then the windows. Ice cracked under the wheels. I opened the front door. The men came in: one large, one smaller. The small man carried breathing-equipment.

'Sorry,' he said, his sharp eyes glancing up at me as we moved through the hall: 'bastard of a night'.

'Yes,' I said. 'He's in here.'

The two men began to unravel the equipment. I relaxed: help had arrived.

And then the smaller man, bending, the mask in his hand, said:

'Look at his eyes.'

4

A chill came to my heart, as though winter and all the ice of the world had penetrated every cell of my body. I shivered. *Look at his eyes.* How did the eyes of the dead look? Now I, too, leaned down. His grey-green eyes were half-open, tilted slightly upwards, and fixed. Your mother, distraught, ran out into the hall and opened the front door, as though to speed the doctor.

The two ambulance men looked at each other; and then at me. Their honest, human, baffled, unhappy faces needed no words. One felt for the pulse in Jonathan's throat. There was none. They turned him fully on his back, and the smaller man began to press hard on Jonathan's chest. How long he worked for I cannot say. Then they tried the breathing-equipment: fixing the mask over that white face, and pumping. The sound was obscene: a piece of apparatus was breathing, but not my son.

I knew it was all pretence. They were merely, for my sake, going through the motions. There was nothing they could do: I could tell by the tilt of their shoulders, their over-active, desperate movements. I went out into the hall. Your mother was in the courtyard, beyond the ambulance. I telephoned the doctor. A woman's voice, thick with sleep, said:

'Yes, he's on his way.'

Your mother came back into the house. I put my arm around her.

'Joan,' I said: 'I think you'd better prepare yourself . . .'

But she would have none of it: it was impossible. Had

he not been laughing, and urgent with life, five hours before?

She stayed by the door, looking out into the court-yard. I went back into the living-room. The two men were finished with pretence. Half-crouching by the sofa, looking at Jonathan, they were helpless; and it showed in their faces.

'Worst part of our job,' said the larger man.

'The worst,' said the other.

'The doctor's here!' called your mother. And there was wild hope in her voice.

He was young, dark, bespectacled; and a stranger. A partner we had never needed to consult. He brought the cold of the night into the room with him. He was swift and efficient, snapping the locks of his black case, lifting out a stethoscope and placing the bright silver disc on Jonathan's bared chest. But I had seen the look passed between experts; and I knew.

He felt for a pulse. And took away his hand.

Silence.

He looked up at me. Again that baffled, angry, human, helpless face. I thought of him scrambling into his clothes, combing his hair, cursing a night call in this coldest of winters; having to leave a warm bed and drive through treacherous ice-bound lanes lit by the eyes of foxes and the white stare of farm walls: only to find death; and to have to lift a helpless face to parents who were waiting for a miracle. (Always the writer's detachment: that feeding upon every happening, however desperate; catching glances, interpreting the set of a face; building the lives of others – always the observer. Now it angered me: telling myself I ought to feel more – not knowing that, like your mother, I was in the first stages of shock, which was to last for days.)

'I'm sorry,' he said. And put the stethoscope away and closed his case.

We stared at the dead face: five people, each with our own thoughts.

The door bell rang. I went to answer it. Two policemen stood under the white porch-light. They looked very young. Behind them the spinning blues and reds: a fairground in a cold season.

'We saw the ambulance from the road,' said one. 'Anything we can do?'

They followed me into the living-room. The house was filling with strangers. Strangers who, collectively, looked down at the silent shape on the sofa.

'A sudden death,' said the doctor, standing now. 'It'll have to be Macclesfield.' He turned to me. 'There will have to be a post-mortem.'

'Yes,' I said.

'I'll fix that,' said the same policeman. 'All right to use the phone?'

'In the hall.'

The ambulancemen stood awkwardly, shifting their feet, wanting to be away. Their business was with the living.

'Thank you,' I said.

'Sorry we couldn't have done more,' said the smaller. He lifted his hands, and let them drop. 'Worst part of our job.'

They left; and one came back.

'We can't get out,' he said to the second policeman. 'Your car . . .'

Now we stood alone with the doctor. Out in the hall the first policeman was speaking quietly into the phone.

'What do you think happened?' I said.

The doctor shrugged.

'Difficult to say. Heart gave out, probably. I don't

know his history. The post-mortem . . . I'll let Doctor James know in the morning. I expect he'll want to call in.'

'Yes.'

He looked down at the sofa, shook his head, said goodnight; and moved out of the room. I left your mother with her arms around Jonathan, and went into the hall. The policeman had finished.

'I've phoned Meadows for you,' he said.

'Who?'

'The undertaker. No preference, had you?'

'No.'

'He'll be here soon.'

Through the hall window I saw another police-car entering the courtyard, tyres drifting slowly on the ice. Doors slammed. The courtyard was now a carnival: *Winter in Sun Valley.*

A senior officer touched his cap with a gloved hand.

'A sudden death, I hear,' he said.

'Yes, sir,' said the first policeman. 'A child.'

'I'm sorry to hear it, sir,' said the senior officer to me. 'Post-mortem, Macclesfield.'

'Yes, sir,' said the policeman.

'Taken all particulars?'

'Just going to do it, sir.'

'Right-o,' said the senior officer. 'No problems?'

'No, sir. Undertaker is on his way.'

'Right. My sympathy, sir.'

'Thank you.'

He touched his cap again, and left. Part of the carnival went away.

The first policeman took out his notebook.

'Now, sir . . .' he said.

5

They stayed until the undertaker came; and then drove away into a night paling towards dawn.

'May we have a few minutes alone with him?' I said.

He was a quiet, good-looking dark man in a dark suit. He looked very clean. There was no trace of tiredness in his fresh, newly-shaven face.

'All the time you want,' he said. 'I'll wait in the car.'

Your mother had gone into the kitchen to go through the motions of making tea. I knelt by the side of the sofa. He was as I had seen him so often: asleep. Mouth slightly open. I pressed my face into the curve of his shoulder and his throat. He was still warm. *A few minutes . . .*

I closed my eyes against the flesh. I said some words of farewell: I can't remember them now.

And then it was your mother's turn.

The undertaker and his assistant carried Jonathan out into the yard while we waited in the kitchen. Still, with all the voices and the coming and the going, you had not stirred.

The three of us sat on the sofa, the undertaker between us. He, too, was brisk and efficient: used to death.

'It has to be done,' he said. 'I'm sorry . . . at this time.'

'Yes,' we said.

He rested a pad on his knee. Pushed forward the point of his gold pen.

'As to cost . . .' he began.

And we talked; and he wrote figures.

'Cremation,' we said: as we had discussed and always agreed upon, for all of us.

Finally he closed the pad and released the point.

'I have to take him to Macclesfield Mortuary now,' he said. 'The post-mortem . . . They don't work over the weekend. It'll be Monday. Funeral on . . . Thursday, unless there are complications. Yes? Altrincham Crematorium. I'll let you know the time.'

'Yes. Thank you.'

He stood.

'I'm sorry,' he said. 'Never seems right, does it: children? You expect it with the old. Terrible thing. We'll do our best for you, believe me.'

'Yes,' we said. 'Thank you.'

I thought of those steep roads to Macclesfield. Over the fells. The car bearing my son away, through ice.

'Take care,' I said. 'It's a tough ride.'

'I'll manage,' he said. 'Goodnight.'

I went alone into Jonathan's room. The bed still unmade, the covers thrown aside. I sat on the top of the small white chest of drawers, my shoes inches off the floor, and looked around. The walls were full of pictures of birds, animals and fish. A bedside cabinet held an inhaler, boys' annuals; a book on how to recognize birds, animals and fish. It was an untidy room; it badly needed decorating. I knew that behind the cupboards and under the bed were dusty metal soldiers and plastic knights, pieces of construction-kits, half-empty tubes of glue, forgotten dice and playing cards, coins and postage stamps.

I remembered how often I had told him that the room was a shambles; that he'd lose his pocket-money unless it was tidied; the times he had come down to the living-

room, hot, flushed, angry, and told me he had finished –
and I had gone up, and nothing much had changed:
everything bundled away in a fury.

Now every crease in sheet and blanket, every dog-
eared book, every picture in danger of falling, every
broken pencil and dried-up colouring-stick, spoke of
absence. I got off the chest of drawers and went out
on to the landing.

As I went past your bedroom, you called:

'Dad!'

I opened your door. You propped yourself on one
elbow, eyes creasing against the light.

'What's been happening?' you said.

I sat on the side of your bed. The ranked faces of
footballers considered me.

'I've got some bad news,' I said.

Blurred with sleep, you looked at me.

'What?'

'I'm afraid . . . Jonathan died in the night.'

You turned your back on me and went deeper into
the bedclothes.

'Are you all right?' I said.

Your head nodded.

I closed the door.

6

The time between his death and the result of the post-mortem was like a landscape visited by a slow-moving, fluctuating mist, settling in the hollows of our days, thickening so that many hours were spent blindly – tasks performed automatically because they had to be done – and then the mist would clear abruptly, and the fact would appear again and have to be faced again: that, not thirty miles away, in a sterile room with successful suicides and the carnage of road accidents for silent company, lay the as yet unmarked body of a person we, and life, had shaped for the past eleven years.

Also, out of that mist that was shock and a numbing realization of how easily breath could fail, appeared the clutter of his days that had to be cleared: the clothes he had worn the day before; his models and his collection of sea-shells; his sketches that enlivened the walls of the kitchen with their charm and obsessive love of detail. Every room of the house held something that was his which had to be gathered up and put to one side, before the sight of them broke us completely.

Telephone calls were made to relatives; and were received. Letters began to arrive; cards with white lilies and smugly smiling angels. Our own doctor came with sympathy and tranquillizers. I found the latter dulled my perceptions, made me sleepy: put a hazy, claustrophobic curtain between myself and reality. I stopped taking them. I wanted to know what grief felt like.

On Monday morning I phoned the undertaker. No, he had heard nothing from the mortuary, perhaps tomorrow.

Tomorrow came, and he called to say that, as yet, they had found nothing: there would have to be more tests. Later that day he phoned again to say that tests were completed, and that we would be informed on Wednesday of the findings. Meanwhile, he was off to Macclesfield to collect the body, and would we let him have some of Jonathan's clothes?

Your mother was so distraught that her sister made arrangements for the consultant who had treated Jonathan in Manchester to visit us. He came the next morning, while you were at school.

He was a grey-haired fatherly figure in correct consultant's clothing. It was not so unusual a death, he said. He had heard of six such tragedies in the past eighteen months. Even he could have done no more than we. Even if we had succeeded in reviving him, might not his brain have been damaged? How did we feel about that bright intelligence dimmed, lost for all time? His words were like thrown ropes, and we grasped them thankfully: only to discover, after he had gone, that they were coming apart in our hands. Nothing could assuage our guilt. We hugged it to ourselves, like a warm coat stitched with thorns.

After he had gone, two calls came through. The first was from the Registrar of Births and Deaths.

'I understand you'd like to hear the result of your son's post-mortem.'

'Yes.'

'It's asthma,' she said.

'Nothing else?'

'That's all it says.'

'Thank you.'

One word for the end of a life: plague, typhoid, cancer, stroke. Asthma.

The second call was from the undertaker.

'Thank you for the clothes for Jonathan,' he said. 'We shall be moving him to our Chapel of Rest this afternoon. Would you and your wife like to see him, before the funeral tomorrow?'

I stood there, looking out of the hall window, across the courtyard to the field. Two cows were stretching their necks to get at the pale winter grass beyond the iron fence.

'Are you there?' he said.

'I'm thinking.'

'Most people find it . . . helpful,' he said. 'We take great care.'

'I'll ask my wife.'

No make-up could hide that agony – not too strong a word.

'What do you think?' she said.

'I'd like to. You needn't – if it's too much . . .'

'No, I'll come too,' she said.

'Yes,' I said to the undertaker.

'Three-thirty all right? You don't drive, do you?'

'No.'

'I'll call for you at three-thirty, then. The funeral will be tomorrow morning, at eleven.'

I put the phone down, not knowing that I was about to undergo one of the most traumatic experiences of my life.

7

Human death had always been seen at a distance. The black hearses speeding through the countryside, followed by one or two black cars. The box, the flowers pressing against the windows, the white faces staring straight ahead. When I was ten and living in London I had seen a drowned man pulled from a canal. The closed, strangely-hued, unnatural face seen at a distance, always remembered. I had not been allowed to see my father at the end. That day I played alone at the Pierhead, watching the Thames suck at glazed, mossy steps; driftwood dipping in the wake of tugs and barges. From the top deck of a bus I had glimpsed an accident: a man was lying in the road near a fallen motorbike. A bloodied face, seen at a distance, before the red blanket covered it.

Now I was to see my dead son, close.

The clean black limousine (also used for weddings) pulled smoothly into the courtyard. There was enough sunlight to begin melting the ice. The day still struck cold. The car was very comfortable. The grieving ride as smoothly as the bride. We spoke of the weather, the coming spring: the scatter of snowdrops seen under the gleaming flanks of the trees.

We drove into town. I tried to prepare myself for something I had never seen. I had thought of death a great deal; even written about it. What had they done to him at the post-mortem? The channels where blood runs away. Professional men, yawning on a Monday morning, as they cut. Elms ticked by, regular as seconds.

And then we were there.

8

We pulled in between a used-car lot and a small, red-brick building which might have been a garage or a place for storing oil-drums. The fluorescent figures on the windscreens of the cars were too bright. We got out of the limousine. The undertaker unlocked a door in the small building, and we entered. There was a desk and a chair and an unlit electric fire. There was another door, ahead.

'Shall I go in first, alone?' I said to your mother. I did not want her to see him if . . .

Her face, hard with too much control, looked away from me.

'Yes,' she said. 'You go first.'

The undertaker unlocked the other door. And closed it behind me.

An attempt had been made to soften the box-like shape of the room. There were flowers and a hint of stained-glass in the three windows. An engine woke in the used-car lot, and ticked over.

In the centre of the room stood the coffin on draped trestles. I moved forward.

The figure of a young boy lay in white silk. He was dressed in a school uniform, and from the top pocket of his blazer protruded the silver-grey metal case of a calculator. White shirt, red and black school tie, blazer, grey trousers, grey socks. Hands by his sides.

I looked at his face.

His eyes were closed; his mouth slightly open, showing

a glimpse of clean white teeth. A faint smell of perfume came from his fair, brushed hair. I went even closer.

I had forgotten how long it had been since he had died. Five days. There was already a blurring about his face: the features imperceptibly merging into each other. I recognized my son, your brother; yet it was not my son.

I put out my right hand and touched his chest. And almost cried out. The cold was Arctic. I had forgotten about the mortuary's deep-freeze. (Since that day I have hated intense cold: the icy metal of fences, the unlit winter mornings; I long for perpetual sunshine, a jungle summer.) I moved my fingers to his hand. Cold, rock-like, carved: like the hands of statues I touched as a child, in parks and galleries. I touched his face. The same marble. His feet in their grey socks: the same. He was hard and unyielding: bitter contrast to that eager, laughing child. Death, you bastard.

My eyes moved over him. I could not understand why the calculator was there. I knew he was proud of it: his latest acquisition – but why was it there? I learned afterwards that your mother, in her despairing confusion, had placed it among his clothes, and the undertaker had tucked it into the blazer. Looking at it, I thought of the Death Ships: the dead king surrounded by his weapons; the Pharaohs accompanied by slaughtered slaves and concubines. A twentieth-century child with his calculator. Its incongruity underlined the surrealistic quality of the moment: the car roaring away in the parking-lot; this inhuman room; this silent coldness.

I looked even closer, trying to penetrate the mystery he inhabited. I wanted to *know*.

It was then that I became aware as never before of the profound division between the living and the dead. The child who had laughed with me; who had run to meet me after a day's work in the Art Room, fair hair flying; the boy I had comforted, chastized, fought with in mock battle; whose bedroom I had entered on Christmas Eve with a bulging pillow-case, hearing his soft breathing in the dark – that child was from another age, another time. This shape in the coffin, shaped like my son, was not my son. It was an almost perfect statue; or a very skilful ventriloquist's dummy: one that would never speak.

The distance between what I had known, and what was now in front of me, was too much to bridge, or comprehend. I was a participant in one of the oldest confrontations of man and the price he pays for living – and I fought for some firm ground.

What I was looking at was a container for life. The shell. That which had made Jonathan my son, and your brother, had gone. The flame was out. The light had died. The bird had flown. Where? Where did the candle-flame go when snuffed? Where did the last sigh go? Where were the notes, minutes after the song, the symphony, had ended?

I leaned down and kissed what had once housed my son. I kissed him between his closed eyes. It was like kissing stone.

The unyielding stillness appalled me. I felt instinctively that I should not have come – I should have remembered him as he was, less than a week ago: alive and vital and running. And yet I knew also that I would not have chosen to miss this meeting: I was learning the lesson. And part of me was glad: he, a boy of eleven, untried, had passed through the last mystery; and in that stillness I sensed in myself the beginning of a perhaps perverse gratitude: nothing could harm him now – no more fighting for breath; no more nightmares; no more worry about school, the trivia of lessons and homework; no more anything: he was free of this bitch and beauty of a world.

How long had it taken to witness all this? The engine was still being tried-out in the used-car lot; someone called, and another man answered. I stood there, wondering whether your mother should come in. Yet we must all learn; we must all face the facts. Better to see, than to imagine.

I went to the door, opened it; and together we went back to the coffin.

Children come from within the mother. A man shares; but he cannot truly know. It almost broke her, seeing him. She spoke his name, and her hands moved over him. She brought no intellect to what she was seeing. She was not concerned with statues or hard flesh or the container for life, the shell. She could never detach herself from part of herself. She saw her son sleeping; and perhaps if she waited long enough he would wake.

'I would like some of his hair,' she said.

'Yes,' said the undertaker, standing quietly behind us. 'My wife washed it herself this morning.'

'Thank you,' she said.

'I'll find you some scissors.'

She opened her bag.

'I have some.'

She cut a lock from the front of his hair. And tidied what remained. That gesture blinded me; and I turned away.

We stayed for a few more seconds. She kissed him. And then we left the room, and the undertaker locked it.

We stood in the outer room. He had switched on the

fire, and the dust on the elements glowed, sparked, and fizzed.

'After the cremation,' he said. 'The ashes. They can be . . .'

'I'd like them returned to us,' I said.

'Certainly,' he said. He opened the door into the street. Cars passed, children were playing football on the Heath; a woman was exercising a dog. 'I'll see you tomorrow at ten-fifteen.'

'Yes,' I said.

'Thank you for all you've done,' she said. 'And thank your wife.'

'We have three of our own,' he said.

And I wanted to question him. I wanted to ask what those years of preparing sons and daughters and wives and husbands for the last journey had taught him. Was he hardened? Was it now just a service? What of his own death? Had the dead told him anything?

But I shook his warm hand and turned towards the centre of the town: the essential shopping; and meeting you out of school.

9

I have never attended a funeral in the rain. Not for me damp and dripping stone angels and spotted stone books, a drumming on umbrellas. There has always been sunshine; and always, somewhere near at hand, an added dimension: a bird singing; a cat stalking a singing bird; an old woman and a child gathering blackberries; a man painting a sign; a jet roaring over, bound for what unknown landfall.

When my mother, your grandmother, died four years ago, I took the train down to London, to an earlier home: walking streets I had known as a child, and which now disowned me.

Riding in the car through streets where old men remembered the old courtesies and lifted their caps, the sun struck the glass with a tropic heat, and I leaned into it, as if for sustenance.

It was the same the day of Jonathan's funeral. I had not expected so many flowers. They almost drowned the raw wood of the coffin. Local farmers rode behind in their battered station-wagons: had he not walked their fields, fished from their ponds; chosen the kitten from among the hay-bales near the grass-scented breath of waiting cows, and borne it home, mewling in the autumn afternoon – not knowing it would outlive him?

The sun struck the glass as we passed over the motorway: the same sun, strong on my cheek – a token, a continuity. For how long?

And once again there was that added dimension: a woman pegging washing on a line, not pausing; a man stooping to tie a shoe-lace, and having to step back as the car took the rise.

Behind us another hearse, a little earlier than arranged, stopped and cut its engine.

The coffin was wheeled down the aisle and lifted and placed on a polished metal strip. We sat and lifted our faces to the priest, whose name I knew, but whose church I had never visited. He said the customary things. We sang the old hymns, remembered from childhood. A sense of continuity. Again, for how long? I looked at the coffin, and thought of that closed face within it; the flames behind the gold-edged red curtain.

Piped organ music sounded, faintly metallic, from a hidden speaker: an age of calculators and Muzak. The coffin gave a slight jerk, a fern trembled and was still; the curtains parted. And closed.

Outside, the air was warm and pine-scented. The woman had finished pegging her washing. People came forward: friends, relatives; his teachers. Hands were shaken, words were said. I looked at the long narrow carpet of flowers. The engine of the second hearse came to life, and purred. Wheels inched forward over gravel. Another priest came out of the small chapel to meet the next death, his finger marking the place.

10

The next morning the door-bell rang. A stranger stood there: a woman. She had heard of our sorrow. She was plainly dressed and her face was polished clean, free of make-up. In gloved hands she carried two books, which she said we must have. They would explain everything. There was no need to mourn. There was a purpose in everything. God had simply called him home early. God needed him. She was almost vehement in her desire to comfort us. Her bright eyes shone with conviction. She *knew*.

I took the books, and thanked her.

After she had gone, I looked at them. The same white figure moved through the same desert. The blind saw. The lame leapt, rejoicing. The same cross stood on the hill. The white figure returned, transfigured.

I read the first page. And was not comforted.

Another woman stopped me in the street the next day. She had attended a spiritualist meeting the evening before. Again I caught that fierce conviction, that missionary zeal.

'I asked about your son,' she said.

I nodded.

'He's happy,' she said. 'He's very happy.'

I thanked her, and went on my way.

11 🖼

The shock was wearing off, but the ache was growing. I found myself setting the table for four. Something would have to be done about his bedroom: the closed door was almost as painful as the open. I found an exercise book with a piece of writing dated a month previously, in his small, untidy writing: *The Best Holiday Of My Life*. A visit to London: a jousting-tournament at the Tower, Regent's Park Zoo, the dinosaurs at the National History Museum. I put it at the back of a drawer, way back.

The undertaker telephoned that afternoon.

'Your son's ashes are here,' he said: 'if you'd like to collect them.'

'Right,' I said. 'I'll be down in about half an hour.'

'I won't be here. But someone will.'

'Yes.'

I got a taxi into town. It was a cold, blustery day. His house was on the main Manchester road, facing the Heath. The taxi waited. I climbed the three steps, and rang the bell. A woman opened the door, and smiled.

I told her why I had come.

'Yes,' she said. 'Come in. They're in the room to your left. On the table.'

The room was a golden blaze of brass and copper ornaments: shining, reflecting each other. A clock ticked quietly. On the large, polished table stood a square cardboard box, tied with thin white string. I lifted it, and found it surprisingly heavy.

I went out into the hall. There was a smell of cooking as the woman came back from the kitchen.

'Found it all right?' she said.

'Yes, thank you.'

She came with me to the front door.

'Will you remember to let us have the empty urn back?' she said.

'Yes.'

I sat in the taxi with the box on my lap.

'Home again?' said the driver.

'Home,' I said.

Alone in the house, I untied the small knots. I took out the brown plastic Grecian urn. Fixed to the circular lid was a narrow strip of black shiny plastic, into which has been punched the words: *THE LAST REMAINS OF JONATHON MARK LEACH*. I thought of the man who had misspelled your brother's name: of his job, back there at the crematorium, day in day out, punching out the misspelled names of the dead as other hearses waited their turn; other fingers marked the place.

I began to unscrew the lid.

I had expected greyness: a small rubble. But there was pure whiteness, like finely crushed chalk. I examined it closely, not touching it: all that remained of a human being. All that laughter, speed, worry, tears, tantrums, the fierce battles with his breath; delight and apprehensions – reduced to this. I made a small indentation with the tip of one finger. The powder gave easily: a mark in tropic sand. I smoothed it level with the same finger. And replaced the lid, giving it a final, quick turn.

12

You remember the small wood at the end of the field, opposite the house? Beyond it are two small ponds, and a stretch of thick grass, thick as moss. You played there often together. Jonathan called it his *Reserve*: there were dry burrows and a fringe of birds' feathers stuck shivering on a tilted stile, and signs of foxes. I had decided to scatter his ashes there; and shrugged back into my coat.

It was colder now, even though the sun shone. There was no heat in it. The field had been ploughed for spring sowing, and the ruts were like iron: frozen, and with runnels of unmoving dry snow. Carrying the box I stumbled across the ridges, and the field seemed to have expanded itself: the wood was a long time coming.

But then I was there, among a silence that ended in a quick whirring escape of wings. Past the thin leafless trees, and on to the ponds, fixed and grey with ice. I stood on the thick grass and rested against the stile. Only one feather remained in the grey-green wood: a rook's, its lustre gone, a ragged black emblem, trembling.

I held the urn against my chest and looked back across the field to the house. He – and you – must often have stood here, looking across ploughed land or wheat or barley or the steaming, grazing cows to where I or your mother had stood, calling you home.

She had not wished to witness the scattering of his ashes. It was too much for her to bear. But, strangely enough, for me it was not something I dreaded doing.

I had helped to bring him into being: I was returning part, or all that remained of him, to the air.

I unscrewed the lid. And, moving from the stile, I swung the urn from side to side: the movement of a sower. The wind took the white powder and filtered it to nothing: it was gone in a trice. But now the heavier ash came, the grey-white rubble I had expected. Some fell to mark the grass; the lighter elements followed the powder. Back and forth I went, until the urn was empty. It was as quick and as simple as that: as the spurt of semen, the spermatazoa racing to lodge and to grow; to become my son.

In moments of love and friendship and laughter I had called him Jon-Jon. And now I said:

'Goodbye, Jon-Jon.'

Said it to nothing that could hear: the steady pulse of the wind.

I replaced the lid, and stood there for a moment more. Then I re-entered the trees, and out again to that iron field, and home.

Early every morning, for days after, I would glance over at the wood, the shine of the ponds. Nothing changed: the view was as it always was – save for a slow coming of new green, and a thickening.

About a fortnight later I went back. The field was no longer hard: the earth crumbled. I came out of the wood and stood on the grass. There was no sign of the ash: not the least grain remained.

Just a warming wind, combing the grass; and flat fields stretching away, under the free air, for miles.

Part Two

How do I begin the journey?
You have already begun.

1

What was destined for two – this book, this letter – is now for one. For you.

I must accept that what I have in mind is pretentious: to give a meaning to a death. Nothing may be achieved. The jungle of my own mis-education may be too impenetrable. But, spurred originally by a glimpse of transitoriness as I watched you both in the garden; and urged on now by the demands of a bewildered grief, the attempt must be made. In fact, in writing the first part, I have already begun.

What is it I want to do?

First, I want to show you from what you spring. So that, in an unforeseeable future, you may be able to say: such a man was my father, less of a stranger.

Second, I want to make something positive out of what has happened. Jonathan's death has forced me to deepen and widen my original intention: he has gone; you and I survive, and must continue.

I think of the dead children of the past: turning plague-ridden faces to medieval walls; drowning alone in ditches beside old battlefields; falling in the perennial massacres; caught in city fires; entering the gas-chambers. All the forgotten faces; the nameless, doused by time. All that potentiality, lost. Of what use were those children: those sparks that glowed for a second, warming a family, then failing and leaving nothing but bewilderment and an emptying of colour from every landscape that met the eye? Why had they come at all, if their time was to be so short? The squandering of nature. Life roars on.

Third, I must come to terms with what his death has shown me. In a sense, I must prepare for my own. There is no morbidity in this. It is as natural as breath. Apart from learning to live, why should I not learn to die?

Not in the old, cramped, life-denying, sin-obsessed, heaven-hoping, hell-fearing religious style. But if I can learn from death, if I can learn to die – then I can live.

2

What exactly has happened?

A child has died. *It was not so unusual a death.* A piece of humanity is dead. Or, rather, *changed.* Has melted again into that same strangeness that was before its birth. Life glitters between two darknesses; or mysteries.

I have written that human death was always seen at a distance. Not so the dying of the rest of creation – not if you live in the country. A city-dweller may acknowledge the fledgling in the gutter, the motionless pigeon in the park, the cat pulled to the roadside – but a day's walk in these fields shows clearer what concrete and stone and neon conceal.

Here is the framework of a bird, bared to the sharp sun, near barbed-wire. A few dirt-grained feathers remain, but the rest is bone, thin bone picked clean by foxes or owls or weasels: each creature moving away in the night, carrying bird-atoms within it, which suffer a change. What is left here, at my feet, is as light as air: made for flight, covered by sinew and fitted with wings and eyes and a cry, it flies no more. It is as still and as quiet as the white plough-stones scattered near it. Tomorrow or the next day even this frail remembrance will have gone, dispersed by frost and rain and wind. Meanwhile, other living birds fly over, calling, and are unconcerned.

Only I am concerned: being born aware.

From within a sea of barley I hear a cry. Treading the

sea, I discover a hare with a broken back. There has been shooting this morning. Even in these last seconds it knows its enemy, and tries to twitch away. I kill it with a stone. The next day it has gone, pulled somewhere. And then the barley itself goes.

I see a rabbit, ahead, on the path. Blind and sick with a man-made disease, it does not move. I prod it with my foot. It stirs, and seeks the long grass.

The pheasants I admired yesterday, today fly into the guns.

My own cat sits on the step, in the sun, and pats a head-less mouse.

In the seas, unseen whales drop.

Through the lattice of trucks, pigs and calves head for the abbatoir, the hooks. I hear them calling in those whitewashed rooms near the supermarket. Their manure is free to local gardeners, who spread it to fatten their roses.

Markers are everywhere, and are duly noted: the bloodied tails of squirrels; the fly in the glorious morning web; the small silver fish in the mud by the lake; the turkey chicks under the infra-red, warm and with plenty of food and water: one has found its way out of the curved tin enclosure, and I help it back – towards Christmas.

We share our world with a thousand other living things: whales, roses, nightingales, tigers and ants. And because we have named them, we think we have them tamed. They move through their own time, keeping pace with us, falling back; or going beyond us. They live as part of the fabric of the world: they are not the background to our activities. They exist in their own right, for the time they are here. Living innocently, instinctively, they do not know they are going to die. And are blessed?

Everything is suddenly precarious, fragile. All will crumble at a touch: trees, cattle, stone, iron fences; this hand. Even the low sun sinking behind the now insubstantial motorway. I step gingerly: what was once rock is now human coral – and even that moves towards a change: to water, and the final elements.

3

And so, it was not so unusual a death. I am surrounded by the markers every day. They predominate at this moment, because I am still in a state of shock, and the dark speaks from every avenue. But they will not dominate for ever. I tell myself this, knowing it to be true. I must find a way out. Or in.

Acceptance of a fact does not kill the hurt. Time heals all things, well-wishers say. Everything?

Perhaps I have begun too soon. Perhaps I should have waited a year, two years. But I know that now is the time, whilst the moment is raw; now, when I am angry and bewildered: facing that blank, rippling mask.

And so, for a time, I turn to the past.

I feed on old newsreels. 1910: the scurrying movements of a crowd at a fairground. I lean forward, trying to read the faces. That gesture, *there,* made over seventy years ago: why do I feel this ache for that down-at-heel figure? That second in time, that wave of a hand, that slight smile. He who made it has gone for ever. I could repeat that gesture every day, running the film again and again. But where is he who made it? What did he do after he left the fairground? How did he spend that evening in 1910?

Where is that girl, and her lover? That leaping dog? That cloud which, even as I watch, disperses?

If we could understand the value of a moment; be fully

aware of the echoes of that gesture, might we not be saved? From what?

Or could we bear so suddenly luminous a minute? Half-blinded by a beauty beyond our comprehension, we would cry for ordinariness, the safety of the usual. It is not that humans cannot bear reality: they have never known it.

4

I have always had a sense of history. Archers inhabit my blood. Even as a child I felt the weight of the past, the press of others who had gone before. I knew that shiver, part terror, part exultation, when visiting castles and dungeons and baronial halls; and the wide, empty, shaken grasses of battlefields. I felt them around me – my ancestors. I heard their cries, screams, laughter, weeping; shouts. I was bound to them, part of the line. They were not strangers.

Once, in the ruins of a monastery, I saw a fragment of a shrine, cemented back into a wall. Only one carved foot showed, but it was enough to chill the blood, and warm it. My finger traced the path of the hand that had cut the stone – and I was there: the air full of singing; the black crows diving from the hill; and the hot eyes trying to see beyond the clouds. And there was that continuity again: monks in the twelfth century, and the boy in the T-shirt, creasing his eyes at hang-gliders.

That sense has deepened over the past six years, since I have known the Old Hall. I go there often, and sit on the hollowed steps below the portico, and look across the wide fields to the lake and the ruined tower, the folly.

Behind me is the Hall itself. In the tall rooms are the portraits of the family who have lived here for three centuries. I look often at those faces. They consider me with unchanging calmness; nothing can disturb them. It is I who now inhabit, for a time, these rooms. It is my conversation that is heard. They are dumb – yet they say everything.

They say that once they were alive, as I am. As Jonathan is not. Jonathan is now one of them. His portrait is not here. But he is part of that crowd of humanity. Of beggars and kings and courtiers and con-men and whores and grooms and kitchen-maids. Named and un-known: racks of dust, hanging in earth.

It was in this house that a child named Robin died on the fourteenth of January, sixteen-seventy-five: dead of smallpox at six years old. A letter of his father's has been preserved. Once again I read it:

Jan 16 1675

Sir,

It has pleased God the one and fortieth night after poor little Robin sickened, beinge Friday the fourteenth of this instant, about twelve a clocke at night to put a period to his sicknesse and life: the indulgence of my good father and mother Pigott was such, that he had what succor, humane policy, and carefull attending invest: but it pleased the Almighty whom nothing can resist to take him I hope to those mansions which excell all earthly Dwellings: we are in greate griefe however for the witheringe of our tender Aprill bud, such is the frailty of our Nature when in right reason we have more cause to rejoyce that he is freed from soe many miserys and troubles that had been necessary concomitants of a longer life; and that now died in such a state of innocency that his greatest sins would not in Christian Charity undergoe no harsher name than sins of ignorance. He yielded up his breath in the same room where he received it, the same day of the weeke that he was borne, and tomorrow will ly at rest in the same church where he was christened: his forward parts had gained much love in the neighbourhood which occasions many to lament his short abode in this world. We have this comfort Though God hath been pleased to lop this tender branch from the decaying trunke, he hath still left a lively bough which his infinite goodness think fitt, may in time fructifie. As I cannot think but my Mother and yourselfe will in some measure participate in the griefe we have for this great losse: soe I cannot but hope your Christian piety will direct you to make use of that patience requisit in such a triall. Thus having disburthened my afflicted minde of some melancolly thoughts I beg leave to subscribe myself

Your most obedient son and
servant
Robert

Preserved too is the poem Robin's tutor sent to the boy's father three days after the death:

Ffarewell!
but who can tell
Deare sir, how soone he may
be forc't to goe the self same way:
Death's a true Leveller: he equalls all
With earth, and when he strikes man's sure to fall.
And what the Doctors could not doe
your God hath done for you:
who sent your Griefe,
Reliefe.

And so it is a strange sort of comfort I feel, sitting on the steps, facing the lake: knowing that another man, another father, three centuries ago, grieved in this house; perhaps sat here also, looking out as peewits called, and geese rose creaking from the olive-green water, to beat and whistle through the cooling evening air: calling, and gone.

We share everything – that man and I – the sense of loss, an empty space which nothing at the moment can fill; a rage that life could end so abruptly, hardly started; that other children thrive and play; that a glimpse of a bird-thin frame and fair hair in town rocks the blood; all the days and the years we cannot share; the unbelief that we shall never see each other again.

We share everything, every emotion – save one.

Of that, more later.

5

Your mother asked, in her distraction:
  'Why us?'
And, in all honesty, I had to reply:
  'Why not?'
We are not something special, who are to be spared.
Yet every death is special.

Another time I found her crying in the garden. She
had discovered a miniature rose which Jonathan had
planted months before. It was blooming: a brightness
against the dark wall.
  'He loved nature so much,' she said.
And again I had to reply:
  'He's still part of it.'

His ashes entered the wind: therefore he is the wind, the
air.
  I breathe him every day.

There are two ways to confront death:
  One is to see it as worthless, a waste: your own ache
sounds through every action, every living thing. The
most banal song that speaks of absence brings sudden
sharp tears. *Why me?* But your ache is sounding through
nothing but your own blood. To nature, and to life, your
special death means nothing. Nothing halts, or takes
cognizance of what has shattered your days. You have
to fight alone, listening to your own healthy heart.
  And you are helped in your fighting if you can accept

that, though your loss is special, your share of death is not. You are one among millions. In the time it takes to write this sentence, another thousand have gone.

And, in other rooms, life is being lifted from the mother, and made to take that first, almost unwilling breath, which may last for an hour, or a century.

It may not comfort you – but it is true. And there is some rock-beauty in that fact.

But it is hard.

6

Walking back from the Hall I use the north drive, which leads to the road and Jackson's farm. To the right is another small wood where your mother once found some grey, antique stone; and in which you and Jonathan used to play, returning muddied and wet and happy. It is bordered by deep ditches, and it was here, not a year ago, that you and he built a rough bridge of branches. It is still there: a framework of mottled wood, darker in rain, now almost yellow in parts; and it has survived the seasons. Two or three of the branches have fallen into the ditch; but the rest remain intact. I step forward and test them. They give slightly: they would not support my whole weight. But they supported two boys; and may still do. Different boys.

Around me are the structures of nature. Soaring trees and rooks and invisible air and sunlight and clouds. But at my feet is something built by humanity: a deserted thing. And it has all the power and sadness and evocativeness of fallen cities and empires. Looking down at its primitiveness, I am back in those stinking times, when consciousness was just a bud in the brain: when hands fumbled in even the sharpening of a stick. It could have been built by the first men to move out of the cave: the need for something apart, a personal habitation, a different roof. It has all the elements of creativity: the need to make. And were it to stay here until the Earth died and fell hissing through space, still it would bear that image: that of men who have paused here, made their mark – and moved on.

And so I move from the death of one small organism –
Jonathan – to the rise and fall of civilizations. That
insignificant clutch of branches becomes every attempt
by man to make his mark before he goes. Yet nothing
lasts. What are we? Are we a desire by nature to contemplate itself? We make our works, either sublime or
frightful, and move on. Tourists lift cameras to headless
gods, shattered temples. Pause and talk of jet-lag over
the immense silences.

I look down at something you and he have made. How
much longer will it remain? Jackson will have to clear
his ditches one day. A labourer tossing the branches on
to a fire. The same ashes entering the wind.

Time narrows. There are no centuries. The same fears,
hopes, desires, rages and agonies – these run through
all humanity, refined perhaps by succeeding civilizations –
or perverted.
    Looked at in this light, the second that Jonathan died
he was at one with Caesar; his death was parallel to the
passing of a boy prince in the valley of the Nile; the
drowning of a wounded Viking; the choking over a thin
bone of one of Earth's first children.

The deserted branches are the deserted temples of the
Incas; and the man who, on this instant, dies in the
public ward (echo of my father), shifts out of living and
into that hard mosaic that is the historic past; and
yet, if we have eyes, the continuous present.

7

I look at life and find it bordered by death. Men and hares and eleven-year-old boys and women and roses thrive for a time; and then go. They become part of recognized history, part of a known past; or – and these are the majority – are totally unrecognized, living out their obscure days, and going quietly, like smoke.

I was going to write that they become part of the pattern, but aside from those two poles – birth and death – there seems to be no pattern. Life is arbitrarily ended; births proliferate, or do not. What justice is dispensed is fortuitous justice. The honest do not necessarily prosper; the devious and the corrupt often do. For a time. But it is all the time we have.

Why did Jonathan – an intelligent, aware, potentially creative child – go at eleven when old, senile, mind-blurred wrecks live on past ninety? Why should idiots survive in locked wards? Why should generals responsible for the wet litter of the battlefield grow kindly and tend their roses? Such questions merit a shrug of the shoulders rather than answers. A shrug of incomprehension, not of dismissal. Never quarrel with a fact. It is as ludicrous as to ask why a certain petal falls before its fellows. It is life, and it is death. And we are stuck with it.

But I am still not satisfied. For my own peace of mind I must press on to some kind of conclusion – to a conclusion perhaps as arbitrary as both life and death.

But to one which is my own: one you may wish to see and know; even if, although we share the same blood, you cannot ultimately take it to your own heart.

Part Three

Are we speaking now of gods or of men?
Why the division?

1

I share with a seventeenth-century father his Englishness, his former home (if not his standing), and his grief; but there is one thing I cannot share – and that is his faith.

I grew in the same tradition, in a society still paying lip-service to a God-ruled, Christ-watched world and universe. After the trenches of France, what little belief my father had, departed for ever. As a child I sat in summer-sleepy and winter-sharp classrooms and churches, singing the old hymns, listening to the old stories, lifting my eyes from the herring-bone pattern of the wooden floor to the wooden man hanging on the cross. And I grew; and, after a while, I put away childish things.

Not, initially, without a sense of regret: it was hard to dismantle a world. But regret became, in time, the joy of liberation.

Now, faced with that still form, that cold silence, and seeking, or making, a way, I turn once again to that old comforter; before I, too, put it behind me for ever.

I have never believed in the sense, or the necessity, of turning to a God in times of distress or affliction: I have never needed that crutch. This is not courage, but reason: that cold, sharp, beautiful lens. Better to turn to a God, if turn you must, in times of intense vitality and sheer delight in the created world: to shout, rather than to plead.

You may be surprised that I want to write to you about religion. But it is part of the fabric, albeit a worn and threadbare one, and deserves some consideration on the way to my own solution (note I do not say salvation) – if solution there is.

(By the way, although unlikely, if you decided, sometime in the future, to become a priest – you would have my blessing. We are facets: and there may be a million universes. I make, and explore, my own.)

I am no theologian, no philosopher. I am a man who has read widely, but not too well. I have had the luck to think, unhampered by academic disciplines. Death shrivels most of the books; tests most disciplines, and finds them wanting. I was trained as an artist, and my teachers did me one great service: they skinned my eyes. And it is with those skinned eyes, I trust, I can look at the idea of God, as I can perceive the design of an ant, the lineaments of a tree, or the bones of a landscape.

2

I live in a society of empty cathedrals, visited more for their architecture than for their spirit. Disused country churches, once packed under the Squire's god-like eye by a dutiful feudal peasantry, are now packed with rows of weeds; outside, the old farming families drown in the long grasses. I live in a time of studied hypocrisy (was there any other?): of bishops who, whilst kneeling to that scant-dressed wooden man, parade their stiff, jewelled vestments. Which is nothing new. We are no longer astonished. It is all part of the game.

There is, however, a tenderness beneath it all – which has survived everything. I am moved – but I am not convinced. I find it easier to understand this world without a God, than to accept it with one. That which has been created, seems to me, at times, more noble than its creator. Notwithstanding Belsen. Which might be blasphemy – if I believed.

What is it that I am asked to believe? That Jonathan's life and death – and yours and mine – has a significance, a purpose: was and is a necessary part of the universe. I do not know if this is true – yet. But whatever the purpose, I do not think it is that assigned to it by those who believe in the God of organized religion, or the heroes of innumerable creeds.

Say the word God, and a hundred fanatics grab your coat. They all know precisely what God you mean:

ranging from the father-figure, stern at times, but ultimately loving, to that bright luminary within a man, which, if dwelt upon assiduously, will survive the act of dying.

I know the Christian religion best. As a child I even won a prize for my knowledge of the Bible.

I am asked to believe in a God who cannot intercede because He values free will more; but who will intercede if prayed to. Who created man perfect, but was shaken to discover His creation had turned away to think for itself. Who will come again in time; or will not come. Who is away, hurt and bewildered, in another part of the universe; and who dwells among us daily. Who, as a last gesture to a selfish race, sent His son – who died for us. Tales of heaven and hell and purgatory. Of wooden crosses that bleed; of crutches thrown down; of stigmatas and vows of chastity and penances and intercessions; and visions in lonely places where the faithful congregate, staring at silent, homely bricks.

It is all so primitive: a vestige of ignorance and superstition. It demeans what it worships. Were I a believer, I would sum up all these ancient elements in one word: *clutter*.

They get in the way.

3

Of one thing I am utterly certain: no man can speak of what God, if He exists, desires or demands of men.

Every word, every action we say or do is filtered through a complex, imperfect being, who will change if a certain drug is administered; if his brain is damaged; or who, if hypnotized, will perform acts at which his conscious self would be outraged.

Whatever created us: you, me, and Jonathan, is ultimately unknown. We wrap around ourselves our little explanations; while, beyond and through us, another, superior drama continues. To say we know the nature of that drama, is to say that the lug-worm understands the mechanics of a space-craft.

Because we are men, we ascribe to a God, man-like qualities. We make God in our image. But to look closely – perhaps too closely, as I did – at the face of the dead, to touch that unfeeling cold, opens up whole universes of doubt, fear, difference; and another, stranger beauty.

4

What we do with our lives depends upon our allegiances. What we believe, sets our course. Again, it is the comfort of the label. Yet all forms of government, all religious creeds, are flakes of straw in a stronger wind than we know. But today is ours.

I am persuaded to believe that all religions began with one fact; and one need. The fact was the appalling realization that everything died. Think of the shock of that discovery on the first thinking man, less than half conscious than we. The loved one does not stir, and he who remains lifts his eyes to the cold spinning of the stars. And places a god in those windy spaces.

Then came the need: to give thanks that he still lived, while others fell about him; and also to humble himself before forces stronger than himself.

We are part of nature, and whales and roses and nightingales die, and ascend to no holy sea or everlasting garden. They die, late or soon, because their time has come. Is Jonathan – or you and I – any different? All the religions of the world are mocked by the hard white grin of the skull, and the silence behind it.

But is that grin the true reality? Do I nail it to my mast like a piratical flag? And if so, have I the courage to accept that hard and beautiful fact?

I have always thought doubting Thomas the most interesting of the disciples.

5

A poor woodcutter has one pleasure in life: his visits to the local inn. He is always reluctant to go home because his shrewish wife beats him. Staggering back one night, he is caught in a sudden fierce snowstorm, loses his way, and falls in a drunken, exhausted sleep on the white earth.

Waking, he finds a priest standing over him: a priest he recognizes as one who had died a few years before. The priest tells the woodcutter he has died in the snow, and must now meet his Maker.

The woodcutter follows the priest through the forest until they reach a large wooden cabin. This is where God lives. The priest opens the door. Inside the cabin is a huge log fire, around which are many angels warming themselves, their giant wings brushing the rafters. The angels glance disinterestedly at the woodcutter, and turn back to the flames.

The priest asks one of the angels to go to the inner room and tell God that the woodcutter has arrived, and is ready for judgment. The woodcutter tries to edge towards the fire, but the angels close ranks.

The door to the inner room opens, the angel returns, and says God will be out soon. Meanwhile, a large pair of scales is placed in the centre of the room, together with a number of weights.

The woodcutter and the priest stamp about the cabin, blowing on their fingers. And then the inner door opens again, and God appears.

He is a weary old man, weighed down with responsibility and too much to do. He is irritated at being interrupted.

'Name?' he says.

The woodcutter tells him.

God finds the relevant page, and makes a tick.

'Correct,' he says. 'Now: your good deeds.'

He can only find one; and a single weight is put in one of the pans.

'Now: your bad deeds.'

The woodcutter winces as weight after weight is placed in the other pan. Soon it touches the earthen floor, and a small hole has to be dug, so that it may descend further.

Finally, the sum of the woodcutter's sins is complete, and God slams the book shut.

'Ignorant, selfish, lazy, despicable creature!' he rages. 'Is this all you have done with the life I have given you? What punishment is too bad for you, eh? Answer me!'

Cold, tired, with the stale taste of too much vodka in his mouth, the woodcutter shakes his head.

'One of your vilest sins is that you cheated a poor woman: gave her short weight!' says God. He looks around him. 'Get me that log, will you?' he orders his angels.

It takes three to carry it. They drop it near God's feet.

'You see this log?' says God to the woodcutter. 'You are to carry this on your back for all eternity. That is my judgment, and your punishment. You understand me?'

The woodcutter remains silent, looking at what seems to be a small tree.

God sighs, and turns away.

'Put it on his back,' he says. 'And don't interrupt me again tonight.'

The angels step forward.

'No,' says the woodcutter.

The angels stop. God stops, and looks over his shoulder.

'What?'

'I'm not going to do it,' says the woodcutter. 'And you can't make me.'

God, the priest, and the angels stare at the small, rough-haired peasant with his blunt, frost-bitten face. No one has ever refused to take his punishment.

'You'll do as you're told!' says God.

'No,' says the woodcutter. From somewhere within him comes a surge of anger, born of injustice. 'Now you listen to me, God. I didn't ask you to make me. And what have you given me in this life? A mother I never knew; a father who was never home to take care of me. Your winters freeze me; I am baked dry in summer. My hands are hard with old blisters; my fingers split, and bleed. I live in a hovel with a wife who beats me for taking a little vodka. Do you know about me? When have you ever helped me? You just make me, and stamp off – leaving me to it. I have to cheat to make a little extra. I long for death sometimes – to get a good long warm sleep. And what do I find? I find you curse me more. Two daughters I have lost; my boots leak; my horse has ribs like fence-posts. Take your punishment? My whole life has been a punishment. I tell you I won't do it. I've had enough. You hear me? – enough! I'm damned if I'm going to hump that log for the rest of time. You try and make me!'

The last words ring out. And the woodcutter, drained of anger, fear moving in, sees, to his consternation, that God is weeping. That old man with the ragged dirty beard is weeping, great sobs shaking those bent shoulders. And the angels and the priest begin weeping now: the great log cabin full of indrawn breaths and tears.

God moves forward and puts a hand on the wood-cutter's shoulder. Pats it roughly.

'I'm sorry,' he says, 'I'm . . . truly sorry. I . . . didn't know: I've got so much to do, you see. So many plans. You're right, my son. I've made it too hard for you. Forgive me. You will forgive me?'

'If I don't have to carry that log,' says the woodcutter.

'You don't have to carry it.'

'You're forgiven.'

'Thank you,' says God. 'Now, do you want that long warm sleep forever; or do you want to go back?'

'Go back?'

'You can go back to the forest. You haven't died. You'll wake cold and stiff, but you'll be alive. What do you want: the sleep, or another chance?'

The woodcutter thinks for a time. After all, God knows now.

'I'll go back,' he says: 'if that's all right with you.'

'Good,' says God. 'Give it another try.'

'It can't be so bad again,' says the woodcutter. 'Can it?'

'Take him back,' says God to the priest. And, blowing his nose, he goes into the inner room and closes the door.

The woodcutter wakes in the forest. The snow has stopped, and a pale milky sun is lighting diamonds on every branch and twig.

The woodcutter runs home, happy and alive. He pushes open the door of his cottage, opens his mouth to tell his wife the great news, and is immediately en-gulfed in a storm of heavy blows.

'Come home at this time, will you?' she screams. 'Take that, you dirty drunken sot! And that!'

Felled to the floor, the woodcutter lifts his eyes heavenwards, and slowly shakes his head.

6

Why should I be attracted to that old Russian story, and remember it so vividly, while others pass out of sight and out of mind? Obviously, because it finds some echo in myself: perhaps some inner, unconscious agreement. It has a reality about it.

Does my creator weep?

Today your mother went to Jonathan's school to see a rowan-tree she had bought, planted in his memory in the 'environmental area'.

And I thought:

For her a tree; for me a book.

Both grow.

7

Remembering the peasant's sudden bitter rage at his own situation – that marvellous upsurge of anger that comes to a man at an extremity, a summoning-up of every inner force, a fierce rejection of fate – I come now to a consideration of our own humanity: yours and mine, and his.

What are we?

We are receptacles into which the lessons of the past have been poured. We are the present state of evolution: a maverick one, perhaps; a burning offshoot that could not be denied, lunging forward, out of line, breeding consciousness: nature's way of giving us an artistic free hand, and the power to contemplate what we make – or what we destroy.

We are fragile, imperfect, afraid; yet we harbour the seeds of strength, wholeness and courage. We have the power to break the mould: to refuse to accept the limitations others have drawn for us, being less hopeful, and less imaginative than we.

We live at less than ten per cent of our potential. We waste our lives with trivia, and stand aghast in old age to find that time has run out and little has been accomplished. Happy the man or woman who realizes early that there is only so much time allotted to us, and that even that is gaining momentum.

Like children we are most free within a framework of love and unforced discipline; and, seeking that security, we turn to religion – and are given our first taste of guilt.

The greatest harm has been done to us by the concept of original sin. This to me is the most scandalous, life-withering doctrine ever dreamed up to explain man's so-called waywardness.

It springs from the absurd notion of a one-time Golden Age, a lost Paradise, a trouble-free Eden. There never was such a time, a sunny haven, or a place of innocence.

We are what we are because we are human: because we dream of perfection, not because we have fallen from it. We are only recently free of the mud, and some still clings to us, but there is nothing dishonourable in that.

I am endlessly surprised and moved by the patience, wry good humour, and sheer bloody nobility of the majority of people set down in a world that is a combination of an abbatoir with a scarcity of humane-killers, and a musicians' gallery where most are playing from different scores.

Who are we, the underlings, to say what has made us, and for what purpose, and as part of what design – if any?

But we are thinking underlings; and are not content, like the rest of creation, to merely taste the day.

8

What has made us we do not know. Merely saying the word God, says nothing. We have fixed a label, lit a light, set up a homing-device: no more. We do not trust silence; and we fear the dark.

Set against the age of the universe, we fill the last second. We have a small grip on this planet; and, again like children, need someone to approve our dreams and explain our nightmares.

For all our technology, our satellites, our witnessing of the event even as it happens – the assassination, the famine, the war, the wedding, the crowning of a beauty-queen, our gradual encroachment of space – we are still shadows of what we might be. Sitting in our polished, gleaming, computer-tended craft, we take into an un-formed universe equally unformed minds. Today's newsreels are the textbooks of our great-grandchildren; and what we now consider achievement will be seen as the counterpart of cave-paintings: beautiful, self-contained, touched with superstition, promising much – but essentially primitive.

This is not to demean what we have done: to see, after an injection, the pain fade from the face of one who has suffered much, is enough to equal the making of a star.

And shall we take into space every man who ever had an answer? Shall we take Christ and Buddha and Socrates and *The Centre For Man's Inner Enlightenment* and the Flat-Earthers and the hardworking Amish with their sinless coat-fasteners and the followers of Transcendental Meditation and the thin health-food crowd and the fire-walkers and the quiet nuns and the flagellants and the witches' covens and white and black magic and the Klu Klux boys and the happy spiritualists and the astrologers and every sect that waited upon a mountain-top for the joyous Second Coming and who trooped down, heavy-hearted, at the empty setting of the sun, only to realize they had calculated wrongly, and that another date beckoned, years hence, glorious and certain this time – and smiled again?

Of course we shall. We shall litter the universe with our approximations, the unripened fruit of our fearful speculations. Refined perhaps, centuries hence; even more exotic. But all springing from one unanswered, and perhaps unanswerable, question: *If we are condemned to die, how do we pass the time?*

9

But are we *condemned* to die? Condemned is an emotive word: it carries echoes of the trial, the sentence. The figure of the judge. Who is faceless.

Are we not, rather, liberated from the dark? It is all a matter of emphasis.

I watch a football match on TV: the ranked, happy, furious, drunken, exultant faces of the spectators. Rows of shouting skulls. Where will all these men and boys be in a hundred years' time?

A voice says: who cares? Does it matter? Is it important? We shall all discover the answer in the end: either in a continuation – mindless, soul-filled; or otherwise: an oblivion of which we will know nothing. You take your breath and you make your choice. Why worry? Forget all speculation: it has crippled and made mad better men than you. Why bother yourself with paths that double back on themselves, and ultimately lead nowhere? Is not the present more important: the laughter of the child that remains; the meal to come; music to hear; books to be written; new lands discovered?

Is not the artistry of that fast, fluid movement down the field sufficient?

But my son is ash.

10

The myths and legends we tell ourselves are attempts to explain what we do not understand. We grasp at what seems plausible and, sometimes, at not even that. Strengthened, buttressed, we feel better able to face the day. Outside, a wilder reality pursues its course: more beautiful, more terrifying, more awesome than we can conceive – never entirely alien, since we are also one aspect of its nature. We are joined to it in some vast forward direction: if we did not exist, it would still continue making and breaking. We are not so ruthless, and we suffer because we love. The reality does not love as we love: it is obsessed with creation. A million moulds are broken every day – in the pursuit of . . . what?

It is obvious that if there is a God which men need to discover, praise, join, and in some cultures pacify, it is a force. A pure rush of energy, which some men call spiritual. It is captured by, and is inherent in, certain individuals who believe they are The Chosen.

But the energy is corrupted by the imperfect being it inhabits, and so the force is tainted, resulting in the weirdest variations. Like faulty wiring it fizzes and crackles: the light is unstable, and the picture only clear for seconds at a time.

Religions, however pure at their source, are soon muddied by successive generations of their followers. As commentator follows commentator, adding his own individual interpretation, each according to his need, the true light begins to dim: is replaced by a five-thousand-watt fanaticism; or is imprisoned in theology and doctrine, and gutters . . . out.

Meanwhile, unhindered, and oblivious of our feeble constructions, our little imaginings, the faceless and the nameless beats on and on . . .

11

I have sat in many churches, alone, and felt that quiet enter into me. The quiet of minds that believed, and still believe. The coloured windows, the candles; the hanging man.

Yet I have found the same reverential quiet in museums and art-galleries. The bones of dinosaurs. The chipped funeral-cases of Egyptian kings. Shells, crustacea; squids hanging in alcohol: evidences of a beginning. The skulls of primitive man: home of the old, ignorant fears. The first rough implements. The gleaming landscapes, the fixed stare of the portraits. They say more to me than the chanting of responses, the age-old rite inherent in the communion-wafer, the bare room where a woman prepares to become the bride of Christ.

Outside, all creation moves and breathes. I cannot force that into one belief or creed. Everything overspills: grief, happiness, the shine of the ponds, the act of writing: my own need to create.

And since other men's gods are not mine, how am I to live? How explain to myself the contrast between the boy who was all life, running towards me (and still running), and that Arctic-cold body that did not feel my kiss?

12

Shorn of the miraculous (the miraculous seen here as the extraordinary – not the daily miracle of simply being alive), Christ's story is still moving: the destruction of goodness. The happy ending seems engineered. Goodness needs no Resurrection. It is like art: done for its own sake. Or the sake of others.

He died, they tell us, believing himself forsaken: a natural, human response to the onset of death; grief at the absence of angels. Then, we are told, his Father interceded . . .

If there was an intercession, then all humanity is saved – *without exception.* Saved from what? From death? Is every dead football crowd streaming home? If that is so, then no one is lost. But no one is ever lost, entirely. The face glows in the mind. The ash coats the wing. Is breathed in, becomes part.

We need no priests. No theology. We are as much the sons of an unknown Father as Christ. Rest upon that certainty as a bird trusts the air.

Our transfigurations are not public.

Part Four

If a rose is unvisited, what use is its perfume?
Show me such a rose.

1 🙢

I am aware of the fragmentary nature of what I have so far written to you. When I write a novel, the words flow easily: one action following upon another, the narrative seeming to unwind from somewhere within me. But this is different. I am finding it hard. I spend hours over a single page, trying to shape what is essentially unknown: my own response to what has happened. There is no story-line, only a clutch at sudden small illuminations; mostly a floundering. And always that desire for a resolution – even though it may crumble tomorrow – so that I may go on.

2

I have heard people say: *I couldn't go on living if there were no God.* Or: *Unless there's a purpose behind it all, what's the point?*

I have understood the human uncertainty that prompted those words; but I have thought it a mean, thin-bodied, essentially negative view of life. An insult to the sweet breath in the lungs.

If there is no God, you still live. (I speak of the God that is named.) If there is no purpose, you make one.

My father and mother lived in a society which considered a young childless couple a source of embarrassment. Why were they barren? My father did not particularly care, my mother did: it was she who had to face the other women of that close-knit community. Eight years passed; and still there were no children. Stifling her natural modesty, my mother consulted a doctor. He examined her. There was a fault in her womb, which a simple operation would correct. She went home and told my father. He didn't care: he left the decision to her. She chose to have the operation. It was successful: four children were born, of which I was the first. I, in turn, married. We had two sons. Jonathan is dead; you survive. Perhaps you will have sons and daughters of your own.

But here is a truly staggering thought: *nature, unaided, had not meant me to be born at all.* Or my brother and two sisters. Or you. Or Jonathan. One woman's decision and a surgeon's skill allowed us entry.

If she had said no: where would be the man who now sits writing at this table, conscious of the hard winter light over the fields, the warmth of his own body, the page in front of him, the music of Bruckner behind him? Where would you be? Or Jonathan? Obviously, nowhere. Uncreated. Lost among the billion unrealized, unripened spermatozoa.

We have slipped in, under nature's guard. We experience the world as a privilege, not as a right. We are extraordinarily lucky: not only did we survive the ten million-to-one death of the sperm, but the womb was changed for our coming. How's that for purpose? Or chance? Or love?

Do you realize what this means? It means that we have been allowed to experience the fact of being alive. Of breathing, eating, observing and loving. Also of falling ill; being jealous, angry, frustrated and desperate. I have always thought it best to consider the cancer as well as the rose.

I still find it staggering that I am here at all. Out of a darkness – which may be another kind of light – more profound than I can measure or imagine, I have been allowed *in*. No matter by whom: God, nature, my mother and father, the surgeon. I am here. Is this the only world? Is this the only life? If my mother had not chosen to give me life, would nature have fitted me in elsewhere? It is difficult to imagine this man, this living, breathing organism as eternally having no existence. But it is more than possible: it is almost a certainty.

Viewed in this light, life assumes the nature of a gift. Again it doesn't matter from whom. I thanked my mother before she died. Behind her, those other men and women, stretching back into a history which is now my own – and yours.

I see it as this: imagine a perfect, black darkness.

Silence. Not even the shuffle of planets and the dying of stars. All senses dumb. A kind of death. And then, suddenly, ahead, the darkness slides back like a panel, swiftly – and there is the living world. Imagine the contrast. There is light and colour and sound and movement. And it is there not simply to be observed, but to be *moulded*. And then, before I have time to grasp the meaning of this world, the panel slides as swiftly back; and once again there is darkness.

If that were the true picture, how we would grasp our life! One chance in a billion to live this day, feel this air, this warmth; create. We would burn our life away; or it would burn us. We are human: we groan at the light of another morning, turn into the pillows and say *another five minutes*. But there will come a time when we will have no voice with which to groan; when another five minutes will be worth every ounce of gold in the world; and behind us will be a garbage-tip of wasted days.

3 🐚

These are pictures and images: attempts to frame the unframeable. Yet they have as much validity as those painted by theologians, historians, scientists and poets.

To me, suddenly, today, it is a privilege to be alive. To have been set down *here*. Because, for all its brutality, its disgusting diseases, its defeated ambitions, its continued ignorance and obvious injustices – all this is played out against a background of much beauty and not a little recognizable insanity. That the world is mad is true. But to live in a mad world which sometimes shows a glint of sanity, of sheer good humour, of sudden compassion, like straws in mud, is far preferable to not to have known it at all: to have remained in that darkness to which we shall all return; although some believe there is another country beyond that dark where all injustice, all unfairness, is resolved. Dissolved? Ready to come again? Or move on? Who knows?

Another thought comes from a contemplation of the human need for fairness: a need for balance and proportion. Is the slow, vulnerable refinement of men – that halting progress towards a half-imagined ideal – also the evolution of a god? Is that God as half-formed as we, and growing alongside us? Are we teaching nature how to grow? Is there within us the half-completed blueprint of a possible paradise?

Yet a paradise without challenges, without something to

fight against, or for, would be infinitely boring. Even as a child I disliked the idea of Heaven: I preferred the scuffed grass of a city park to the prospect of eternally shouting *Hosanna!* to a golden light.

And always that word *God*: how it clouds the glass.

4

Strange how thin is one's composure.

Today I went to the Art Shop in town. It was still closed for lunch, and waiting outside for it to open was a woman who works there as a part-time assistant. I had never spoken to her before, but we began talking. She told me she had to work because her husband had recently died, and she had two daughters at university.

'I hear you have lost your son,' she said.

'My son has died, yes,' I said. 'In February. He was eleven.'

'My son died at four and a half,' she said.

'Jonathan went so suddenly,' I said. 'At nine o'clock he was laughing and playing around. At three he was dead.'

'My son went even quicker,' she said. 'Alive at eleven o'clock; dead at ten past. Killed in a car accident. People don't understand, do they? They try. Have another child, they said. But you can't replace the one you've lost.'

'No,' I said. 'Have you any religious faith?'

'None at all,' she said. 'You?'

'No.'

'You find the strength inside you,' she said. 'You have to – or you go under.'

'Yes.'

We looked at each other. We knew what we shared. We were no longer strangers.

'You get something from it,' she said. 'You feel for others.'

The shop opened. Another assistant served me with tubes of paint, and brushes.

As I entered the small wood at the end of the road, the first tears came for over a month. Tears at loss and at absence; human vulnerability; mixed with an anger at the indifference of the day: how everything went on, oblivious, uncaring.

5

Let us consider the possibility that you and I are completely alone. That, mingled in the tide of evolution, we grew one difference: consciousness. And nothing more. That that consciousness, sublime, liberating, frightening, alone separates us from the rest of creation; and, like the rest of creation, we come, we spend some time, and we die; making way for others of our kind. And the hairs of our heads are not numbered; and no one sees the sparrow fall, except ourselves. That however fine may be our creations: music, art, drama, architecture; that however beautiful may be our approximations to a guessed-at truth: law, medicine, religion, love, they are devised and formulated against transience and cosmic indifference.

It is no good saying we know, one way or the other. We don't. We paint our own backcloth.

Yet what we believe affects our living. Do I want to believe? Believe what?

If the universe is a caring one, it cares less than the consciousness it has created. Or *differently*. It shows no sign of grief. Shares nothing with me. The landlord is absent.

I see no reason to believe that the universe cares, as humanity cares. And I can use no other standard of reference, being human.

If I died tomorrow, the universe would not notice my going. I would be absorbed, as the ocean absorbs, accepts, the raindrop.

I am a grain of dust on a planet which is a grain of

dust in a universe composed of other grains of dust: some burning, some dead.

I am deliberately playing it down, in order to paint the starkest picture possible. Only by facing that kind of heartlessness can I continue.

Yet this insignificant grain of dust – for which, as a separate entity, the universe cares nothing – can mould that universe to its own design. It seems to me that I have inherited a drop, an infinitesimal share, of that force which makes mountains, super-novae, and ants. Given a space of time – in which we do not destroy ourselves by war or unchecked disease or an end to the Earth's resources – you and I, as the *personalization* of that force, have the power to invest that creation with the one aspect it lacks: a desire to hold and examine; to contemplate what it has made, rather than to hurry on; perhaps even to love. Are we the outriders, the scouts, of a journey towards love? Are we the first fragments of *caring*, hung like fireflies in the dark?

In other words, and I find this intensely difficult, and may be entirely, profoundly wrong:

Whether by design or by an accident of evolution, with the advent of man – sullied by ignorance and the trappings of fear – there came that quirk, that perhaps uncatered-for child of consciousness – *human love*. And it is that *extra* to creation that stands hurt and baffled at the place of death: looking down at something for which the universe does not care – one more lifeless star, one more empty shell to be ground to dust – raging now that such a thing should be so: not content with those precious past years we did not realize were precious; but, being human, wanting children and sunlight and breath to go on, for ever.

6

Everything is held within the limits of my mind. I want that mind to be clear, forceful, cutting: like the beam of a laser. Instead, it is the product of an unsatisfactory education; shaped by a society whose gods are not mine; affected by mood and hangovers; hung about with echoes of misrecorded history; and run through still with inherited primitive emotions.

And so I am aware that everything I write is conditioned by what resources I have; and even those are in part made and restricted by the age in which I live. I am caught between the destruction of old, empty myths and superstitions, and the haphazard building of others which, in turn, when other men live in this house, work these fields, will themselves change.

But in my search for a temporary strength – since there is no security – I am aided by one aspect of myself in which I have grown increasingly confident over the years, and that is – intuition.

I love facts and I distrust mysticism. (One beautiful thing about consciousness is that we make our own paradises, our own hells.) Yet I trust a formless thing, deep within myself. When I act according to my intuition, I feel relaxed. I know I have acted according to the unwritten laws of my own nature. It is when I go against it, for the advantage of the moment, that I feel edgy and contemptuous of myself.

That is why I cannot go along with organized religion; why I avoid spiritualists, fundamentalists, evangelists, group-therapy sessions and the annual naming of another Messiah from whatever backwood. They don't feel *right*.

What, then, does?

Is what we feel about the world purely a reflection of our own needs? If we need a god, one appears. If we can live without one, we deny, or ignore, its possible existence. If we like ice-cream, we eat it. If it causes our skin to erupt, we avoid it.

Yet, when something as earth-shattering as the death of a loved one occurs – how, then, do we react? To what, or whom, do we call upon? Would we eat ice-cream if there were nothing else?

How do I distinguish my need from my intuition?

That is where, reading that sentence, I would throw the book across the room. Dryness is settling in. Outside, frost glitters. I dislike semantics. I settle for the intuition. Goodbye analysis.

7

This morning, re-reading what I have written, I came to:
I thought of those steep roads to Macclesfield. Over the fells. The car bearing my son away, through ice.

And the black car came back, and the white face torn from me. And I never knew grief went so deep; or that I held so many tears . . .

8

One dark night, in the past, a woman came to the house, carrying the body of a cat. Behind her was the shadowy form of a man.

'Is this yours?' she said.

I looked at the cat in the light of the porch. Black and white fur, the head lolling and strange.

'Yes,' I said.

'I'm terribly sorry,' said the woman: 'it shot straight out in front of us. There was no time to stop. We got out and . . .'

'Yes,' I said. 'It's good of you to come and tell me. Others would have driven on. I'll take him.'

His fur was wet, and her empty hands gleamed.

'If you'd like to wash . . .' I said.

'No, thank you,' she said. 'We have some Kleenex in the car. I'm very sorry . . .'

'It happens,' I said. 'We've lost three since we've lived here.'

'Goodnight,' she said. The man nodded.

'Goodnight,' I said.

I lay the body on a sack in the coal-shed, and went in and told your mother.

The next morning I told you and Jonathan.

'That means we can have another kitten,' said Jonathan.

'They have some at Carter's,' you said.

And I thought then how familiar with a kind of death you and he had become.

After you had both left for school, I went into the shed. The cat was where I had left it: its white fur startling against the black coal: those gas-filled, flame-filled lumps of pre-history. I stood, looking down. There was little blood. I thought of its life: farm kitten, lost and mewing at first, hiding under chairs; growing, chasing butterflies; lolling content in summer grasses; tracking mice and dropping their headless bodies at my feet; noisily lapping milk; stretched at full length in front of the fire: the coal ignited now, the gases roaring like the small far roaring of a humanless past, a dead forest warming both cat and family; the purring, the snarls, the scratches that came after too much teasing; how it waited outside Jonathan's bedroom before breakfast: to enter, and settle.

Gone now: all that half-wild activity.

Its body was as hard as wood. Holding one leg I carried it like a stiff cat-shaped bag to the back of the garden.

Who cared? Not the universe. Even you and Jonathan were contemplating the arrival of a new life, a new individual.

I buried it near to where I had buried the others.

Tall grass stands there now; and the new kitten is grown, and, as I write this, sleeps in front of the fire, another burning forest.

9 ❧

So, it is possible that we are alone. Cats and men: exercises in forms of life. Something needs to create, and go on creating. Of its own momentum? Blindly? Searching? After many false starts, still not satisfied? Are we an experiment?

Cats and men go down: other men come; children run to another farm to view a swarming basket, and to choose.

If the universe does not care for the now lifeless child, the unmoving animal, who does? The believer says God. I see no evidence of that. I say: you and I. Against that indifference we go on as if life mattered, trusting in what? Each other? Rarely. Rather in the movement of the blood, the beating of the heart, the warmth of the skin; freedom from pain. And, if pain comes, we turn to God; or to that inner strength which is born of an angry obstinacy: a rage that says: *Do your worst, you bastard: if I go down, I go down shouting.* Or laughing. Or full of a terrible bitter silence. Like my father.

But why bitter?

We are thankless. The possibility that life is a continuous experiment, of which we are a temporary side-effect; or the most successful outcome yet; or merely the cooling dross left by a force now concerned with other, perhaps more sophisticated forms – a force which does not care as we care – this frightens us. We need to feel we are important. We need reassurance: we want life to fit a human frame. One that echoes our own preoccupations,

our sense of right and wrong: what we feel to be
fitting.

Always life on our terms. Because we have, or know,
no other? Even if our terms are petty, terms that shrivel
when confronted with what we see outside our windows:
the daily rebirth of the sun, and possibly ourselves?

10

I mourn Jonathan because he was just beginning. Just getting into his stride. When my mother died four years ago, at eighty-three, I felt nothing like the ache I feel now. Eighty-three is a good age, and she was tired and ready to go. She desired an end, or a new beginning. She had seen wars, and the rise and fall of governments; she had heard the same speech from different mouths, year after year. She was tired of her body: it had turned enemy, no longer companion. She slept a great deal; and now she sleeps forever. That long, uninterrupted sleep which, if she did wake, would have passed as a single night.

But the death of a child is harder to take. I, who have lived longer, know what he has missed. True, he has missed pain and frustration, and the violence of the mindless; cold, and not having enough money to buy warmth; love not returned; the sight of other people's empty lives which is an almost equal pain; life which will not budge even when taken by the throat and shaken.

But he has missed something else. I will not make a list. You name it . . .

It is now ten months since he died; and every morning I look across the field to that patch of green before the ponds. Seagulls were there today, driven inland by the first hard days of winter. Whiteness against the dark trees. Soon it will be Christmas, the first Christmas without him. I promise myself, and him, that I will cross that field at night, on the Eve, and leave something: an orange wrapped in foil, or an apple. Then I shall return to the house and put your present by your bed, hearing your breathing; and leave, and pass that other, empty room. It will be tough.

But I will gain some comfort: knowing the apple will be eaten by a chilled unknown animal or bird. And nothing will be left: the bright foil gone to another field, another part of the country.

11 🐚

I am trying to find an old equilibrium: one that I knew in the past, that left the night Jonathan died. Notice I do not say *an answer*. I am trying to find a point of balance on a very fragile bridge, as the ropes fray.

Something has entered my life which was not there before: a continuing, daily sense of loss. It fluctuates: coming painfully strong at times – when you laugh in a certain way, as he laughed; or still discovering something that was his: a dusty badge down the side of an armchair, a book with his small, thin signature – at other times it is a presence on the periphery of things: but always there.

I realize now I have rarely been unhappy. I have been *less* happy many times; but never desperately unhappy. I am, and always have been, an optimist. I once saw a book whose title *The Answer To Life Is No* stopped me in my tracks. I had never thought that there was even the slightest possibility of saying *No* to life. The mere fact of staying alive was an affirmation.

Even now, with Jonathan dead, the ache ever-present, the ponds glazed with ice, I still know days when I feel everything is possible: when it is obvious to me, though there may be no other life than this, that I am glad to be here.

Then it comes to me that though I am alone, unaware of a watching, caring, emotion-feeling creator, I am still sustained. I am held in a shuttle of breath and a pulse of blood. I cut myself badly a week ago, now there is hardly a mark. I am defended. Just as, after last night's fierce gales, the landscape outside this window appears unchanged (no doubt there are dead trees down and branches scattered), so everything works for a continued preservation: a marshalling of forces so that the organism may survive.

For what purpose?

At its lowest (or highest?) the reproduction of its kind. Was my mother's decision, and the then state of medical knowledge, and the skill of the surgeon – was all that purely fortuitous?

Yes.

And Jonathan's death?

Painfully (since humanity needs reasons):

Yes.

12 🦚

Death is built into us. The last fail-safe. It is inherent in our birth; and it is the border to our lives. There may be a time in the future when death itself will die: when for every failing organ, a replacement is speedily grafted into the system. But there is something repugnant in the concept of an unnaturally extended life. A man needs to die as well as to live. He needs to re-enter the flow; or to know Heaven or Hell; or to go into oblivion: what you will. I do not believe life is a preparation for death: that old grey teaching. Life is a preparation for the fullest enjoyment of the next minute; but to be aware of death is to appreciate the never-to-come-again worth of that minute, free of the dark.

That is one of the lessons of Jonathan's death, or of any other death – man, lover, cat, hare, or rose.

Even if his death was fortuitous, what arises from it is not. In other words, we construct from our disasters the means of dealing with that disaster. And, thus armoured, move on.

13

How far have I progressed? – if you can call a continuing return to preoccupations a progression.

The fact that all our births and all our deaths are fortuitous – although what rises from them may not be – still does not lessen the sense of loss, or compensate for a life abruptly ended. It is still too early: the armour not thick enough.

I believe that Jonathan – *as Jonathan my son* – now exists nowhere but in my own mind. I could be quite wrong: but that is what my reason tells me – and I have not the faith to believe otherwise. Others tell me to leave reason aside: that the spiritual life is comprehended by other factors, never by the intellect. But I love reason; and the idea of my personality, or any other, continuing for eternity, appears impossible; and limiting: I want to try other universes, other forms. If I close my eyes I can see Jonathan. He will never age. A child will accompany my last minute, as he now accompanies my every breath. All who live with the memory of a dead loved one feel a measure of guilt. Not enough was said; not enough was done. It is a natural, human emotion: born of a certainty that that face, that body, will never be seen again – as *that* body, that loved face. Dissolved. Loaned to us; taken back. Reformed? Reshaped?

The lesson is obvious : *say it now, do it now.* 'See you tomorrow,' I said, that night. Tomorrow may be too late.

14 🦋

The created universe will sustain as best it can that which it has created. Until it can hold no longer; and then it will let go. It will take back into itself the dead container of something that briefly illuminated the world; or, in the future, if man survives, outer space. And where goes the illumination?

Back to the source.

But not to the source that is contained in the Bible or the Koran or the Talmud. It is not there. Labelled, imprisoned, confined, it can do nothing but shrink itself to a form acceptable to man's comprehension. Named, it is robbed. If it is pure energy, fastening upon what it can develop and discarding the rest, what of it? Is it any less marvellous, less mysterious? Is not the dance of atoms as awesome as the coming of angels?

We are fed dry, packaged, name-branded husks; while, outside us, and inside us, there is all the sustenance we shall ever need.

15 🌀

I mourn my son because I loved him, and now he can never realize his *human* potential. And who is to say that he, or his essence, is not beginning elsewhere: free, perhaps, of the limitations of that humanity? I don't know – but the thought is attractive, offers a rough comfort.

But supposing he is as dead and as unreturning as the rest of a creation that has its time, and finishes – what then?

Then I have been fortunate. I helped create a being that tasted life for eleven good years; I shared that love. My mother could have said no; the surgeon could have been less skilled. I could have been lonely, unproductive. Instead, I had Jonathan for eleven years. And you are still with me: and, because he has gone, are more precious.

If it is the nature of life that, of necessity, it leads to death, and none are exempt, then, after the tears and a lessening of the ache, it must be accepted as the price we pay for taking that first breath. It is harder to accept the death of a child. But it happens. And though you cry an ocean, he will not return.

He has gone where we shall all go. Meanwhile, how can I go on living? How can I continue, having witnessed the death of all my care; and seen my own end?

Part Five

I have lain awake all night,
wrestling with the Great Question.
I also.
Were you blessed with enlightenment?
Yes, I have decided to plant lettuces
rather than cabbages.

1 ❧

After my first novel was published, I had a letter from a reader who liked the book. He was a retired naval officer who now farmed in a small way in Wales. Our correspondence grew; and, a year later, he invited me to stay for a week in August. Out from the hot city, I entered quietness and a grey-stone house which was full of books; a white bedroom overlooking a courtyard; a view of bare hills circled by hawks; and civilized talk under stars and the hunting of owls.

The second night was full of rain; and, in the morning, I stepped out into a beaded, shining, sky-reflecting world. It was down at the end of Small Field that I saw something that has stayed with me ever since: as clear and as sharp and as bright as that morning.

The rain had swollen a wide stream, and the water raced, bringing down from the hills the small debris of twigs and grasses. A movement to my left caught my eye, and I turned.

A long lance of knapweed, which, in drier times would have stood curving, free and undisturbed, over less busy water, now found its head caught and pulled by the flood. It moved for a time with the flow; then, held by its root, it sprang up, its head spraying a scatter of drops – only to dive again into the stream; to be pulled, to rise, to scatter; and once again to enter the flood. The movement was circular and regular. A green wheel, spinning silently.

I sat on a low stone wall and watched that steady, pulsing circle for a long time. And it came to me then, and still suffices, as an image of creation. Of a silent green wheel that drives on, or is driven on (I do not ask now by what or by whom: it is sufficient for me that it is there, free of tablets of stone, of the laws of men): on, through the whole of what we call time, space, history or life.

True, once the level of the stream had dropped, the plant would once again stand free; but for the time I watched it, it was a visual counterpart of a force which, once started, cannot stop.

It was an image of unceasing, unwearying life – a *promise* – and, as such, I have treasured it.

.

2

That hurrying green wheel generated, and generates, every living thing. In what way are we, as humans, different?

Since what has made us is intent on making, it appears that with the coming of consciousness, came also a sharing. Not only did nature desire to contemplate what it had made, it gave to one aspect of that creation the opportunity to escape the bonds of instinct, and to become what it was itself: an artist.

The shares are not equal. There is Mozart and there is the pianist in a down-town night-club. There is El Greco, and the pavement-artist who copies El Greco. Some are given too little, and the heart aches for something it knows not what: a hidden country from which they are forever barred – in this life, which may be all they have. Others, the visionaries, are given too much, and are broken by the terrors of the present, and the impossible beauty of the future.

3 ❧

As a child I could never reconcile what my eyes saw and what my mind imagined. I was always aware, from the earliest, of a hidden beauty – and sometimes frightfulness – behind the commonplace. It is only now, looking back at that boy wandering city streets and parks, that I can put into words the unspoken dissatisfaction I felt for what I had inherited. I felt I had only to pierce the ordinary to come into my real kingdom. I thrived on fantasy, which is only another aspect of truth. I told lies, tall stories, and was thrashed for the trouble they caused my parents and neighbours. Yet I believed the lies and the stories. They were more real to me than the sharp-voiced classrooms; the drunken men singing themselves home; the piled litter of the market, where a crumpled red tissue marked *España* set the mind racing. I told myself I was not my parents' son: I had been given to them in trust by my aristocratic father, and at twenty-one (or perhaps tomorrow) I would come into my own. How else could I explain to myself the rage I felt at a world everyone else seemed to take for granted, even to bear with?

There were times when that world changed: when, helped by sunlight, an everyday wall would blaze, and dusty ivy was transformed into something more than itself; when a face seen in a bus was Helen returned, and the Thames a new Mediterranean; when, playing in that patch of grass behind the house, I would look up from beaten grass to see light wink on a high airliner, and my heart would go with it, to the Incredible Islands.

A little later I discovered liberation. I found I had a talent for drawing; and I could create my own land-scapes, no longer restricted. I read a great deal: the local library became my second home. Then came music: a half-heard snatch from a record shop, freezing the blood. And, rising above bad teaching, came poetry. Art won me over.

I had discovered what set that green wheel spinning: a desire for change; for experiment; for new forms, new excellences. It whirred on silently, within myself. I was wedded to whatever had created me. At once the world clicked: like the last piece of a jigsaw pressed into place. Not that I was less dissatisfied: the bus moved on, taking all that beauty away; the airliner touched-down without me; the ivy dropped back into shadow – yet I knew now why I was here: I was a maker, not a destroyer.

4

But now, for a time, the jigsaw is broken. Death has swept the board, scattering the pieces. That which I helped to make – a living, breathing, artistic, aware human being – is no more. Fact follows fact – I agree with all the evidence, and can do no other – millions have known the same pain, and will continue to know it: but it is hard to bear.

It is obvious that the so-called spiritual nature of man is of the same branch, the same essence, as that which makes a man an artist rather than a priest or a believer. That an artist is also a believer is also obvious: but he believes in the totality of life, in total freedom to create, and he will not press all that exuberance into the thin confines of a creed, a theology, a doctrine. He needs to be as free as that force which patrols the universe; and perhaps as ruthless.

I write a book; I make something which before did not exist; I send it out into the streets; and, while others are reading it, I have half-forgotten it: being involved now with the next. And I never get it right. Always what is produced falls short of the original intention. Earth-shattering beauty; deeply-felt insights; belief in the essential freshness deep down things: all trim themselves to neat lines of words on a page. And are as confined there as any god held in a disciple's teachings.

Is it possible that that which created us knows, or feels,

the same frustration? Imagine the desire I have to make something perfect as being an infinitesimal part, a grain, an echo, of the all-consuming drive, rage, love, passion that forces itself into every structure it can find; and having made it and set it living, roars on. This would explain the diversity of forms in which life glows. The final imperfection being death? Or the same materials used again and again: moving towards an excellence it, and now we, set ourselves?

5

A TV and film-makers' club in Piccadilly: watering-place for the creators. Lunch over, I spoke to an old friend about how far I had come.

'You're still postulating a religious view,' he said.

It was almost an accusation: as if I had betrayed him.

'Am I?' I was full of fierce denial.

'You may have dismissed God,' he said: 'but you're still speaking of purpose.'

'And you?' I said.

There, among the empty coffee cups, he looked at me.

'Function,' he said. 'That's all we are: functions. There doesn't have to be a purpose.'

'And Jonathan?' I said.

'Has ceased functioning,' he said. 'Hard to take – but there it is.'

'And can you bear that view of life?' I said.

A middle-aged man, divorced, infinitely weary, he lit another cigarette and sat back.

'Another coffee?' he said. 'Or how about a brandy?'

6

Functions?
Hurtling home in an express Inter-City train that night, darkness outside strung with lines of orange sodium lamps swinging over unknown towns and the headlamps of cars; commuters asleep, heads back, mouths open, going home to children and women loved or not loved, mortgages and overdrafts, plans for the summer, hands resting on evening headlines, the night's viewing packaged and coloured, until tomorrow and tomorrow ... I leaned my head against the cold glass.

Was that all we were? If it was, I could bear it. It was a thin, cramped, mechanistic answer, but if that was it, so be it. No arguing with a fact. A function named Jonathan was no more. A glitter of laughter and warmth – eleven years of speech and running and looking at nature: tragic, but there it was. Enjoy it while you have it: heroes share the same dust as tyrants. A mature man braces his shoulders: there is even a hint of nobility there.

A drunk came weaving through the train, carrying a six-pack of lager, his bemused, slightly sweating face fixed in a smile.

'Happy Christmas, pal,' he said.

'And you,' I said.

He made his smile wider, and, keeping his balance, weaved on.

I thought of his destination: the house, the lighted windows in the dark; a key fumbling for the lock; smell of food. Faces lifted. *Welcome home, function.*

7

It is not magnificent enough. It is too drab and lifeless, a denial. I can't fit myself into it. If all I am is a complex function, then I shall transcend it. I will not be contained. The circuit may be programmed for death, but allowance has been made for creativity and growth. I refuse to accept my limitations.

What is it that wells up in us when a certain piece of music is played; that shivers the spine when a collection of words on a page is read; that causes an intake of breath as the road dips and the coastline shows a fret of waves?

Awareness.

Awareness of what? Beauty? The half-happy, half-sad impossibility of ever knowing it completely?

It is a response of a deeper self. There is no denying this. It is the essential core, the reality. Even if it is only a manifestation of a higher grade of organism, a glowing of certain fibres in the brain: it is *there*. A diamond discovered among the swill of most of our days. The Janus-face of cruelty and oppression. The fact that the fibres will dull and fail at death is no matter: the response is there, today; and, if acted upon, enlarges our appreciation of what it is to be alive *now*, at this second.

And that enlargement of the second, when time is no more, is, so the mystics tell me, to live in eternity.

But I am no mystic. I have known times in my life

when I have acknowledged – usually in an old house, heavy with memories; or alone upon some headland visited by successive raiders; or staring at a flint arrowhead in some out-of-the-way country museum; or in that ruined monastery in Wales – that there are moments, usually seconds, when I *am* the raider, striding up the shingle; or the monk aching for a sign; or the primitive man lifting his head to the sound of devils in the wood: when I see that time is a man-made restriction, and all history is packed into that instant. But then the demands of my own time intrude; and I am back with day-to-day preoccupations: bills, health, ambition – what you will.

I have no wish to sit in a cave, with a wooden bowl for alms; see no merit in joining a religious order where natural needs are tamed and the soul is picked clean as a bone; have no desire to be part of a commune where all is wholemeal bread and meditation before the regular sunrise: I love the noise and the clatter of humanity; the faces in the street; all the unknown, guessed-at lives, which I remake. I have grown to love the insecurity, the fact that nothing is promised: that though I may head for disaster, the coin may spin and fall the other way, and the clenched fist open like a rose.

8

Art, then, is my province. Awareness the natural growth from which it springs. I shape my own response in the interval between two darknesses. But of what use is my art if, in the end, I am to join the silence of all who have gone before: Caesar and Jonathan, Beethoven and Alf Kirkman – an unknown boilerman I knew, gone wifeless and childless and drunken into the same mystery – of what use? To an artist such a question, even if it arises, is left unanswered – is deemed unnecessary, an intrusion. He needs to create as others need to breathe: the joy is in the making. But what of the man, resting?

My first response to Jonathan's death was shock. Then came anger. Then came grief. Then, together with grief, came a need to put something into that emptiness. To be engaged upon something which his going precipitated, and made necessary. Hence this letter to you, this book. There is a satisfaction in the growing number of pages: they build *another* Jonathan – extension of himself.

What, after all, is art? It is a man's need to create. And, other men, seeing that creation, feel better able to live.

A world empty of art is barbaric, and will die sooner; and deserves to die. We may be a temporary mark upon the universe: a brightness that winks for a second among the whistling of meteors, and which no other eyes acknowledge. We may have the potential of giants: and, if we survive, great art will go with us as we leave the

Earth and set out to colonize space. Beethoven will be heard, and Shelley read, and Rembrandt hung in those airy complexes of the future. Earth will then be seen as that green mother of a stupendous civilization. Or become a dead clinker where once, for a brilliant second, a strange, vulnerable race called men made music; until the music was drowned and the experiment written off.

9

Great art, then, is immortal. Even less-than-great art: the street-songs sung forever. Not so the artist or the singer: he is as dead as the tramp discovered in a ditch this morning. He, like the tramp, has moved on. Or not moved on.

But for the majority of people their immortality rests with their children: that frail linkage that stretches from the hidden past and into the equally hidden future. All buildings will collapse; all bridges will be replaced; worlds will be discovered, used, and then abandoned. Clutching their videos of the Collected Works, the heirs of today's commuters, football crowds, and refugees, infiltrate the galaxies.

Why do I concern myself with pictures of an imaginary future? Why cannot I simply enjoy this moment? What *is* this moment? Its elements are these: a good night's sleep; a good breakfast; there is a pale winter's sun throwing my shadow on to the wall to my right; the room is warm; I am in no pain; the pages grow. It is enough for the artist. But not for the father.

I am living Jonathan's time as well as my own. I am breathing air he should be breathing. But in saying that I realize I am breathing the air of all who died before their time.

Or was it their time? In one sense it was: there is no plan in the dying of children. Or of men and women. We do not go when we are called. We go halfway through a joke; or waving as we cross the road; or choking on a peach-stone; or alone with a handful of tablets; or reaching for a book; or dog-paddling towards a crowded lifeboat; or quietly, while an ambulance tries to find a house, and a father is dressing.

Losing a son, I gain the weight of every other parent's grief: reports of the deaths of other children cloud my days as once again I relive, and share, the same disbelief.

Therefore, as buildings collapse and worlds are abandoned, I must be willing to let him go; even though I am unwilling. What am I letting go? At its most rarefied: a link in the chain to the galaxies. His absence will never be felt, or noticed. A thousand such chains are broken every hour. The wheel whirrs on. But, on a human level, I am letting go a portion of myself, and the promise of a mature individual, who might have done something great with his life. I am left a clutch of memories: which is not a work of art, but an untidy collection of days and evenings, and rain-filled after-noons crouched over games.

Pages are colder than human blood; the finest prose shrivels before that delight, that sudden, spontaneous laughter: the dice tilting, falling, showing the needed number – home and dry, at last.

10

Strange how a glimpse of the dark can offer us a sudden light, an unexpected illumination.

I remember when I was twenty and living in one room in London, I used to walk through Hyde Park to Speakers' Corner. There was something about that patch of ground under the trees: that collection of battered lecterns, faded banners, hoarse-throated madmen and icy fanatics. It was a cauldron of despair, laughter, prayer, derision, and sometimes violence: joined to a shared appreciation of what frustration can do to men and women. There were men who knew they were God; fierce-eyed tramps whom a past injustice, real or imagined, had made deranged; a calm, precise man who talked of his conversations with visiting Venutians; a wild-haired woman who stood apart, playing a violin, and cursing all who came near: all this going on under the green leaves of spring, the unconcerned mating of birds; and, later, under white stars hung about the branches.

One Sunday evening, around seven, I stood listening to a monk describing the devotional life. The crowd around him was small: he made joy sound boring. I looked away from that intense stare, those white hands against the green, and prepared to move on. And then was stayed.

A girl stood a little way into the crowd, looking up at the monk, the small crucifix, the brass Christ. Her

face was pale, and very beautiful: as if some inner fire
had burned away all excess. Dark hair crowned a pair
of large eager eyes; a straight nose, a half-smiling full
mouth; a classic throat. She wore a tan raincoat, collar
up, and tied in a loose knot at the waist. Hands in her
pockets, she listened while I drank all that beauty in.

The monk finished, and launched into a final prayer.
The girl closed her eyes. I moved closer to her: feeling
a terrible desolation that soon she would go, and be lost
forever. A few scattered Amens sounded, and the monk
thrust the crucifix into his robe. The girl turned away,
tall, hands still in her pockets, shoulders slightly
hunched, moving towards Oxford Street.

I knew I could not let her go. I had to speak to her;
to know who she was. I caught up with her as she
waited for a pause in the traffic.

'Excuse me,' I said.

Backed by the first lights of the night, that face which
was at once cold and yet burning, looked at me.

'Yes?'

'Look,' I said: 'I've . . . I've never done this before. I
saw you in the crowd, over there. Would you have a
drink with me?'

The eyes looked beyond, or through me.

'Why?'

What could I say? I was a young writer abroad in
the greatest city in the world, yet I stumbled.

'I'd . . . I'd like to know you. You can say no if you
like.'

'I don't drink,' she said, her eyes now on the constant
flow of cars.

'Coffee?'

She looked at me. Close to, half-lit by headlamps,
shadowed, lit again, it was an ache to move my eyes
over that throat, those lips.

'All right,' she said: 'I'll have one coffee. Where?'

'There's a place across the road,' I said.

We ran between the cars to the island; and over again.

We sat surrounded by plastic: cups, tables, decor. I told her about myself: the room above a Kensington square; the shouting ballet-dancers in the next flat.

'And you?' I said.

'I'm a nurse.'

'Where?'

'It doesn't matter.'

'You won't tell me?'

'No.'

Time passed; she refused another coffee. She must go. I asked her if I could see her again.

She said no; but that I could walk with her to Hyde Park Corner.

Out again in the cool spring night, waiting to cross into Park Lane, I asked her why I couldn't see her again. Looking away from me, down that wide avenue bordered by magnificent hotels and the dark of the park, she said:

'Because I'm going to die.'

The coughing into the handkerchief, the red spot glowing, ruby-like, in the white folds; the clutch of a white hand; myself wandering, Dante-like, through the courts of the world, seeing nothing. Nothing but this face, inches below me.

We walked down Park Lane.

'Die?' I said. 'What's wrong with you?'

'Nothing,' she said. 'I'm very healthy. Unfortunately.'

'Then why are you going to die?'

'Because I want to.'

'You *want* to?'

'Yes,' she said: 'the sooner the better.'

'But why?'

Outside the Grosvenor, the doorman standing behind us like a prince under the yellow light, she turned and faced me. And now there was an added fire in those eyes, those cheeks with their aching bone-structure.

'Look around you,' she said.

What could I see? A city that was waiting for me to unlock it. I loved the rich shuttle of the cars; the hotels only the wealthy could enter, and which one day would open for me. There were books to be written; jungles to be hacked through; deserts to cross; women to be known and loved: perhaps none as beautiful as this.

'So?' I said. 'It's life. What's wrong with it?'

And into that face came a sudden, terrible weariness. The light dimmed. She looked away into the shadow of the park.

'I can't wait to die,' she said. 'I can't wait to get it over with. I don't want to go on.' She half-smiled. 'I don't want a relationship with anyone.' Then, with a swift vehemence, she said: 'Can't you see how sordid everything is? How stinking rotten all of it is?'

'Don't you know you're beautiful?' I said.

She dismissed my words as if they were a hindrance, a net of unnecessary lies.

'Don't start that,' she said. 'Let's keep walking.'

In an instant my whole conception of life came under question. A beautiful girl, surrounded by the shine and the glitter and the promise – and some sordidity – of the world, of a great city, *wanted* to die. I couldn't believe it: it was a pretence, a dramatic stance occasioned by too much night-duty, the phlegm-clotted calling of old sick men. I suggested this to her. She shook her head.

'I've tried,' she said. 'Three times I've tried. But I know now that that's wrong. I'll go when Christ wants me.' She looked up at me. 'You see: I'm His.'

We parted at Hyde Park Corner. I watched her walk down the bright interior of the bus, and sit down. A girl eager to die. She did not wave. The bus entered Piccadilly. I turned towards Kensington.

It was then that I was made aware of an extra dimension. Behind the massive façades of world-famous stores, the motionless models, the scuba-diving displays, the travel posters for the States and the Islands of the Pacific: the bronzed girls stretched on surf-boards – behind all these was a darkness which, to some of my own kind, was infinitely preferable. I knew the deepness of an eternity others wished to enter. And I was stunned and appalled. To me it was a perversity, a negation of everything I held dear: the beautiful fact of being alive, of sharing in the experiment.

It would round off the story to say that later I read that the body of a young nurse had been found in the Thames. But I heard nothing of her, ever again. She never appeared again at the park, though I looked for her.

But I shall never forget the intensity of her desire, even *love* for death, or the idea of death. It was my first introduction to a hatred of life; and that pale, burning face often intrudes – and I wonder about her. Unknown to herself, she had made that evening more than itself: not darker, not depressing – but full of a sudden, surging beauty that, in the end, in time, and upon reflection, proved even more achingly beautiful than she.

11 🙦

I have never believed that love alters not when it alteration finds. There is no virtue in a blind consistency. We must change or we do not develop. Nothing is static. Love either grows or declines. People who stand as firm as a rock in all weathers have the same deficiency as rock: they lack imagination.

This is prompted by hearing of a local man's suicide. Leaving no note, he went into the depths of a wood, and drank wine with the tablets. I can understand his need; can even applaud his courage. There was a time, a black moment, when I thought of following Jonathan: the child alone, out there in the totally unknown. I wanted to share the dark with him, stand by. It passed: I convinced myself the human son slept the long, forgetting sleep. I could not assist what remained, if anything remained I could name – being without a greater understanding. And my business was with the living.

To commit suicide is to deny a worth; or, in despair, to seek one. Can I envisage myself doing it? Easily. I have enough imagination to acknowledge the power of my own suppressed anger at the lunacies of life. But I am not consistent: today the lunacies are merely laughable – part of the peep-show, the Big Crazy Parade; God's own joke: allowing us the choice of the punch-line – going out to applause; or propped against a tree, surrounded by birds who sing without knowing; and drinking the last of the wine.

12 &

The first Christmas without Jonathan. Your mother decided to spend it away from home. She could not face the prospect of placing presents by your bed, whilst that other room remained unvisited. On Christmas Eve you and she left for Chester: I was to follow the next day. Strangely, I felt that to go was somehow to desert him: that he waited over by the ponds; waited to be called home.

On Christmas morning, early, I went across the field to the grass and the ponds. I rested against the gate. There was thin ice on the water: three brown leaves were held, motionless. Complete silence: the road deserted, no sound from the motorway. Standing there, the cold working at my ears and my cheeks, I knew the same emotion felt by those who worship their ancestors, who trudge at dawn through wet grass to a high point where a ramshackle platform holds the mummified father. Gifts of flowers and fruit left to rot. The need to feel a continuity. A refusal to completely let go.

I put the apple on frost-fringed grasses. I had nothing to say. There was no one to hear. A gesture. I looked back at the small farmhouse, a hundred yards away from my own home. A Christmas tree glittered behind steamy glass, backed by a line of greeting-cards. The old festival. A starling came and grasped a branch. The thin tree shivered; steadied. The starling waited, feather-ragged in the cold. It was welcome to the apple.

I walked back slowly, ice cracking under my boots.

Three days later we returned to the house. You were unwell with a heavy cold, and went straight to bed. I found myself going to your bedroom often, and quietly opening the door. I had to make sure you were still breathing.

13

A few months ago I went back to the streets of my child-hood. Little remained of what I had known: a church, hemmed in now by tower-blocks; a war memorial with a stone Christ blessing a kneeling soldier; a few plane trees; the gateway to the docks. Night came, and I walked down a street I had lived in for years. All the memories: the terrors, the delights. The house had gone: unseen motors hummed behind a blank wall. But the old lamp-standard was still there: lit. Reaching the end of the street, I looked back. There was a cold mist off the river, and I saw the boy that was me swinging silently by an old rope, as he had done in the past: the creaking strands tightening, then unwinding.

I sit back now, and listen to the music of a dead composer. He who made that melody ate, slept, went for walks, raged, loved, wept, despaired, laughed; and reached for another pen. Gone now: a rack of bones in another country; the brain that had housed this symphony no longer burning in that empty skull. Yet the music remains. I hear what he heard. The child still remains: swinging through time on a creaking rope.

We are commentators on two worlds: the outer and the inner. Both prevail, continue through time, but are changed by the habit of the age. A medieval man's inner life bred demons and the fear of hell. And ours? Still primitive: unable to control our own aggressions;

unable to seize the glory which religion once promised, and the electron microscope hints at.

Nothing lasts. Jonathan slipped through my fingers like water: which was my, and his, breeding-ground. Up from slime, to what?

To a desire to continue. To continue making. The mainspring of art, however unconsciously felt: to halt, for a time, this rush of atoms to an unknown destination. To make something that will last for longer than a human life. At least while men need music. At least while boys swing on ropes.

At least while the ash that was my son, and your brother, glows somewhere in the fire of the sun; or dusts an empty planet.

Part Six

But surely the universe itself will one day die?
Not my universe.

1

It is almost a year now since he died. His birthday is approaching, and also the anniversary of his death. What do I feel now? The same emptiness, tempered by a realization that others fare worse: today I read of a fire in which four children died, all under eleven – the parents spared. Spared for what? How will they bear the silence?

How comparatively serene my life was, before that night. Death had touched it slightly; but not with this hammer-blow. It still reverberates; I am still recoiling.

That first object to be venerated, man's old friend and father – the sun – warms this winter window: and I wish with all my heart that it warmed him.

This letter must end somewhere. I will end it on the second of February, a year to the day: I have always worked best to deadlines.

Even I acknowledge the neat brutality of that last line. Does the fact that I do not erase it bespeak a new hardness?

2

Perhaps life is a continual thickening of armour. And those who do not harden, either go down or exhibit their scars like medals. Again, that's too bloody neat.

Have I hardened? A friend once said to me: *You have a talent for survival.* Have I a growing indifference? Am I becoming like my father: dumb with shock from the trenches, the frame of life forever askew; compassion replaced by callousness: the stronger the light, the darker the shadow? I look at newspaper reports of the latest massacre, stinking fruit of some crazy nationalistic feud; and turn to the night's TV: the Western, the chat-show, the old classic movie. To dwell upon those black words, to stare too long at the face-down clutter of bodies, and to admit the inferences: I am ripe for the funny farm.

Yet, equally, somewhere, another father surely mourns? Or, equally crazy, shouts that his son has died a glorious martyr.

Is anything worth a death?

And so, we come to the nub of the matter: the worth of a death.

Your mother cannot understand why I should write this letter to you. To her it is inconceivable that I should, so soon, while the pain is still with us, daily come to this room and immerse myself in such a contemplation. I have already said why: as a believer turns to the cross, I turn to those sturdy, time-polished counters – English words. I like to look at what I am thinking. And I am thinking how I can handle the death of a part of me.

3 🍃

I have not accepted his death. Is any death acceptable? That of the pain-wracked, perhaps; of those who have had enough; the tortured who gladly seek that sweet oblivion. Though others tell me he lives elsewhere, I believe he does not. Not as Jonathan: the individual I helped to make. What has been given back (taken back) is an essence of life which has no name, is no longer housed in anything I would recognize. The form has gone. I have to live the rest of my life in the knowledge that all I have is eleven years of memories; a few photographs (which I cannot look at, yet); and assorted drawings and writings which hint at what might have been; and are evidence of some delight and awareness at being human.

What is the worth?

The worth is an enlargement of myself. I am not speaking of the nobility of suffering. I have always had a horror of the self-inflicted wound – the pain pilgrims feel, going on their knees up a rough track, towards a clean, kissed shrine. I see no merit in sainthood; and the Stations of the Cross have no place in my world.

But an unexpected window has opened; and beyond it is a new landscape which, though still marked by withered trees and gaunt winter-struck gardens is, even as I watch, slowly losing some of its bruising chill; and, ironically, may in time be visited, for the sake of its own strange beauty, as often and as easily as that other country: its pulsing, colourful, summerful neighbour, the land of the living.

4 🪷

Looking at children, what is valued is their unthinking spontaneity: their immediate response, unaffected by experience. Such a response is a constant reminder that life is ever fresh: reborn every day, every minute. But, just as childhood has its benefits, so also does maturity. They are harder won, but more lasting; and ultimately, richer. What must be learned is that ideal equilibrium: the potential of the next, unused hour; and the tacit acknowledgment that it may be your last. Once you have understood and accepted that – you are free.

It seems to me, now, that death can only enhance life: *if it is allowed to.* Death is the salt to living: if tomorrow we go into the dark, how achingly poignant is today.

It is true that in one respect life has no intrinsic colour. The field in which lovers have lain; a murder has been committed; a crop has been harvested; a man has attempted suicide; a boy has seen a hare: this is known differently by all of them. Yet it is the same field, with its own nature, unaffected by what emphasis successive lovers and murderers and farmers and failed suicides and delighted boys give it. So too with death. After the natural shock, the event, now neutral (always neutral?), awaits our interpretation.

It can cast us down for more than the necessary period of mourning. It can blight our days, so that we exist forever in that chill, unexpected land. It can whisper to us that life is ultimately meaningless. If what awaits us at the end is our own obliteration, and the same grief we now feel is transferred like a disease to those who love us, what is the point of going on, of ambition, of rearing children who too will one day fail and fall? It can hang like an albatross about our necks; or enclose our hearts in ice; or change us so deeply that even our closest friends turn away. At its worst, death has taken one life; and is offered another.

And yet it can enrich us. We can live for those who have gone. We can pack into our lives that extra time the dead have given us. For they *have* given us time: the expanded moment that comes when we realize that, for us, the blood still moves; the world is still there to be explored and made over; that, for now, this minute, this hour, this day, we are free of pain and hunger; that, though we still mourn in the deepest part of our being, death has liberated us, has made us see the transitory nature of everything; and life, being transitory, is thus infinitely more precious; commanding more attention than ever we gave it when we went on our way, still unthinking children, before death opened our minds, sharpened our eyes; and set us free.

5 ❧

Last night was the coldest of the year, and this morning you were out in the courtyard, sliding on the cobbles and marvelling at the icicles hanging from the roof and from the mouths of drainpipes. I could see, and feel, the pain in your mother's face that you were alone out there. I am coming to accept that there will always be, even in the happiest of future times, a patch of numbness in our lives: a sense of absence, which, others tell me, lessens in intensity.

You called me out to see spiders' webs rigged with frost. They hung from the fence fronting the field: it is a reflex action now to look up and over, to make a silent greeting. It was very peaceful over there: straight lines of frost-covered fields latched by thin black trees. Unaccountably, I felt a sudden wave of happiness, for which I could find no reason.

Sitting here now, on this first day of a new year, a new decade, I watch sparrows drop from the spiky framework of winter bushes, to take the crumbs we have left on the coping. Beyond the garden a mist hides the farmland, marked by one bent tree. I feel, instinctively, that this letter is drawing to a close. I have crossed and re-crossed the same patch of land; going back over my tracks, and again returning. This is an interval in my life; and now I must go on. I am not entirely reconciled. Death is a bastard: robbing us of those we love, taking away their future and changing our own; but, like the man standing near the ruins of his storm-wrecked house, there is only one possible reaction: to build again.

6

In the more secure past (or a past that appears more secure to us, shadowed as we are by the possible total destruction of our kind; our future entrusted to madmen who are never concerned with the individual: a past composed of communities linked by jolting coaches in which only the privileged rode, leaving others to know intimately a few fields, a duck-pond, the superstitions bred by a boundary), when a father addressed his son in a letter there was much morality woven between the lines giving news of family, the failure or success of a crop or a business, the birth of a brother, the death of a grandparent.

Not so with this letter. I am not concerned here with how you spend your future (your present is my present): for this was written from a need to make something out of a negation; to replace an emptiness; to discover an attitude; and for you to understand, when you are older, an incident in your own history.

The fact that you may disregard any hint contained in these lines doesn't worry me. This is not a polemic; not propaganda for a certain view. I am concerned only with a human being's discovery of another's mortality; and consequently his own. I address it to you, because we share the same root, the same blood. And, in time, the same dilemma.

What now do I fear?

I fear that future days may dull this sharpened perception: perhaps we live most fully when we are being tested.

I fear my own kind, and for my own kind. I fear fanaticism: men who *know* they are right, and who will kill to prove it. I fear the mob, and cherish the individual. I fear that what we have been given – the basis, the foundation, the beginning – and all we have so far shakily built, will fall away from us for the sake of words on a banner. Above all I fear the death of difference, the absence of eccentrics; the metal future: machines which, once created and set humming, will allow no deviation from the programme.

I fear for grass: trimmed and tamed and contained in squares, and which cannot be walked upon . . .

7

What have I discovered?

I have discovered the ache of loss, the coming of a deeper grief than I thought possible. I have witnessed the extinction of a personality, and have been made to face the continuing certainty that never again shall I see that loved individual. I have discovered the transitoriness of all things; and their consequent worth whilst they are with me. I have discovered the uncaring nature of the universe; and yet, as a living entity, I am sustained in an attempt to permit me wholeness. I have discovered that men make religions out of their own limited apprehensions of their world; and that, outside their own imaginings, exists a mystery which they can never name, only trust. I have discovered that tragedy need not diminish those who suffer it: that it has a positive aspect; and that, having won through to some kind of angry acceptance, brings a more realistic view of life, and a deeper resonance.

8

What have I learned?

I have learned what is important. That, faced with the ultimate, things move to a correct proportion. That every day free of pain is a bonus. That there exists in myself acres of my nature which are still undiscovered: one has been opened by grief – what others may be known in the future, sprung by a more disciplined art, or travel, or meetings with strangers? I have learned to be wary: the time that is left is savoured now, dwelt upon, treasured. I have learned compassion: I know what it is to mourn. I have learned, too late in one respect, that I have not cared enough. And now it is too late: for him. But not for you. I have learned the strength of my own creativity: that, called upon, it never fails to respond, and joyfully. It rushes in to heal; and for that I am grateful. I have learned to expect death; and though I resent its intrusion, I grant its cold necessity.

9

What do I believe?

I believe I share in the making of the universe, perhaps many universes. I am engaged in a stupendous working out of forces, the nature of which I have only the minutest of understanding; and yet know intuitively that I, and even the smallest atom-fizzing rock, are somehow part of an experiment which is in its first, possibly uncertain stages. I believe in life; and my belief is strengthened by death. I believe that somewhere there exists an answer, but that the wrong questions are being asked; or even that no question is needed. I believe it is not what happens to a man that matters, but his opinion of what happens. I believe to laugh at life is better, and saner, than condemning it: the experiment may be the work of a mad scientist, but to die laughing is not a bad way to go.

And I have always believed, in life, the best is yet to come. I cannot speak for the other side, the dark.

10

I had planned to finish this letter on the anniversary of Jonathan's death. I have in fact finished it three weeks earlier. Life, and growth, for humanity is never that well-rounded. Things are finished before their time; or in a time which runs on other rules than ours.

And so, Martin, I come to an end. You know a little more about me than when you began reading. Yet I am still hidden, even to myself: life is a shifting, tremulous thing, elusive as quicksilver. Part of me resides in you; another part is scattered with the ashes that was Jonathan's shell. Being human, I am still hurt. Being human, I am not reconciled; yet part of me soars.

If there is a light after the dark of death, by the glow of which I shall know and be known – fused to the lost part of me, all tragedies explained, all wounds healed (that old human longing for love's extension) – then I am content to wait and see.

But I live believing the opposite: that I have been granted a certain time to walk about this Earth, and to take a look at its marvels and its follies – and perhaps contribute to both – and what I do *matters*: if only because I can do no other – being set going, my heart ticking, my blood running. And then a transformation, the nature of which I do not know, but trust, since all humanity has gone before, and will go: borne upon an air I have loved, circling my home, the Earth, and moving on . . .

But I am in no hurry: I have things to do. Death can wait awhile.

Or not wait.

11

I shall go downstairs now and get my coat and take a walk across the field, to the grass and to the ponds, and stand there for a moment – and then walk on to the farm and get some eggs.

I may, since the day is cloudless and the end of winter seems at hand, go even further . . .

Coming?

A000011269861